COLLECTED POEMS

Greg Luti

gregluti.com

Copyright © 2023 Greg Luti

ISBN – 978-1-7340110-0-5

Edited by Greg Luti

Ilustrations by Yuzhar Ramadan

Cover Art by German Creative

Preface

I wrote this collection somewhere between the years of 2017-2018. I only got to finishing a few years later as I was working on other stuff in my life, mostly a blog that I run, which although the articles are not that long, is tougher than it looks to run. One day, I finally remembered the collection of poems, and frankly the blog articles were getting stale, so I decided to finish what I had started.

I stopped writing this book, and editing the poems once they stopped speaking to me. As if the poems got tired of me revising them over and over again. At a certain point I have to let these go into the world, with all their faults and potential.

Concerning the title, is one that is a simple subject. These poems are just that to me, collected. Over a few years of time, I wrote them and put them together. Only in the past year have I gotten to adding the images and other minor details that make a book presentable.

The poems are all over the place, as my inspiration from them vary. I do hope that the reader can find one or two that they can take with them as I have done with other poems I enjoy. If that is not the case, I added a few images, that they may like. – Greg Luti

Table of Contents

COLLECTED POEMS

Right

After all, that was done.

After all the lies that were spread to every mouth and mind who knows tales and thoughts.

After all the newspapers articles that wrote columns, the online blogs that gave their opinion to anyone who would read it, and the news updates at ten every night.

After the books of him written by generations of people and publishers and read and memorized by all the school children.

Books that wrote of his dishonorable and disgraceful lifestyle.

After all the times his name was brought up in conversation in dining rooms of families, kitchens of friends, and rooms of strangers to make a point for how one should not live their life.

How an outlook, a perspective that agrees with him is wrong and shunned upon.

After we long bury him in the ground with an unmarked tombstone and no funeral.

After we spit on his ashes and shed no tears of his passing.

After his grave is unrecognizable by dirt and decay and is removed for others without any resistance.

After we remove his statues from the city squares, his names off of the schools, hospitals, and any other center once dedicated to him.

After cities and streets are renamed to a more appropriate title.

After the protests in the streets, the wars in different countries, and the chaos, madness, and sadness brought upon by those for and against him.

After all that is of him is negative, and not a single note, a single line of him is positive.

After all of it.

When there is no more left to hate of him, to laugh at him, to ridicule him.

When the comedians run out of jokes on him.

When the writers run out of stories with him.

And the scientists run out of studies about him.

When all that is left of him is a legend, a myth, that can be easily mocked or disregarded.

When the world comes to believe he never even existed, that he was a character in a story to teach our children of liars and thieves and all those naughty people in the world who are shamed for their behavior.

That the man was not a man, who walked this Earth and lived as others have.

After it is accepted that a legend is all he ever was, and shall remain to be.

After his legend is replaced by a more contemporary example suited for a new crowd that views his legend as outdated and bland.

After his name is deleted from the history books, poetry books, and every other book out there.

And the time he lived is never spoken of again.

His friends, family, and enemies are banished from our world with him.

After there is nothing left to say of him.

After we forget about him and his life.

It turns out; he was right.

He was right all along.

Becoming "That"

A lot of writers around the world in every country and all languages spoken by a man in the past, present, and future want only one thing from their words.

For people to read them.

For audiences to take some time and read some of what they worked hard on and put their heart and soul in to complete.

Some writers get lucky, and that happens.

Readers stop from the daily hassle that life throws at them to read a few words, to glance through a few stories.

Other writers are not so lucky, and they are the only audience their book ever receives.

Then there are "those" writers.

The ones who are more than writers in our world.

The ones we talk about when we bring up writing.

They reach the popularity that is almost unsettling to an extent.

It is either a credit to their genius for being able to touch so many readers with their great prose.

Or a result of right timing, and business savvy on their end, or perhaps both.

They have movies made of them, by actors who look like them, by actors who don't look like them and by every actor in between.

Books written about their books, of their impact on our world, how the writer came to such a revelation in words, how we should marvel at their genius.

Signs are made with their pictures and quotes and hung from any wall in a library that has room for them.

They are the answer to the question, "Who is your favorite author?"

A question that is asked in our society to understand oneself and others better.

I saw someone once with a tattoo of a quote from a writer.

That is the level we are talking about.

It is not just a book and some words.

He is not just a man with some words.

People use their words to live better lives.

That is a strange phenomenon right?

Is it me here?

Am I wrong for questioning the legacy of those in the field that I wish to be in?

When your popularity is to the point where your contributions come to define aspects of our world, the reality is frightening.

Because you are no longer a writer with a story to tell.

All writers want people to read their works; they dream of publications as much as the stories themselves.

But that other level, when your words are that well-known, that popular, that read, is just strange.

Ironically we all want it.

The Road Of Isolation

The same reason you are great is the same reason you are alone.

You have come to defy the standards in your field, to rewrite the rule book.

All know of you, from here to Spain, those that don't love you for your innovation, admire your status.

Even your enemies, those that mark you on their walls and curse you every morning blaming you for all the wrong in the world, respect what you have done.

Yet...

Here you are again.

In the same spot, you've been in for years.

You are no closer to any other human now than when you started.

Your mistrust of others has led you down this road of isolation where self-reliance is your only response.

So much that when you find someone who you do trust, someone who likes you and wants what is best for you, or god forbid the person loves you and wants to spend their life with you, you push them away.

You don't need anybody.

Not now, not then, not ever.

That's how you look at it.

You'll do it all yourself.

You have come into this world alone, and that is how you shall leave it.

Well, congratulations, you have done just that.

You are as lonely as one could be.

You know not of the love of a wife or the heart of a family.

Nor of good times with friends.

Or even the content comfort one feels by liking himself.

Not a day goes by that I don't pray for you and your happiness

I hope that despite all odds, that you change, that perhaps even if it is for a brief moment, you are happy with who you are.

The world does not know this of you, nor they ever will.

Even if they do, they will reject these flaws for you are their hero.

The one we all wish to be because of your success.

No one wants a hero whose personal lifestyle is that of a common lost man.

You will never find happiness in this world if you only focus on yourself.

Unfortunately, that very outlook is the same identity you have come to flourish under.

No matter how much you are alone, all the empty rooms you sit in, all the moments you miss, you accept this torment as if you are a cursed man never to know love.

The real hurt that breaks you is the same that makes you.

I know you won't listen to me, but I want you to know that it is never too late to change.

You may not know it, or even see it, but you can still be the man you always wanted to be.

Leaving This Place

You ever notice, when you take a moment and look around at all the world has, from the mountains to the sky, to the cities and people, how we all seem to be leaving this place?

We can't wait to leave our world.

Our world, the world we dominate is one we are happy to punch a ticket to ride somewhere else.

Whether it is through a virtual world where you play as a character as real as you are, with friends and family, and special tasks and events they must attend,

Or an afterlife, where you die and your soul, the part of you that is your main essence, leaves this world.

Geez, we are here for five minutes, and then we go?

Why?

Why do we go as soon as possible?

Maybe our curiosity is more than a mere curiosity that is to be overlooked.

Maybe there is a reason we want to escape this world and then inevitably do.

Is it me here with this speculation?

Am I overthinking two unrelated topics and apply philosophical principles where none belong?

Like a person with a mental health condition seeing patterns in random objects that are not there.

Pardon me, if that is the case.
Questions are all that fill my head some day.

As technology develops, you will hear people ask what reality is?

How can I tell the difference between fake and real?

If I were fake, would I know?

If I were real, would I know?

If we say that this is real, but then find similarities between our world and a fake one, am I still right in seeing myself, my life, and my experiences as real?

Some scholars will bring up Plato's *Allegory Of The Cave*, and how the shadows are metaphors and the real story can be applied to today as much as for an Ancient Greek audience.

This story is made to comfort you, to let you know that your confusion of life's reality was asked by a man thousands of years ago, and it turns out, after hundreds of wars, books, and generations, we still don't know.

The audience may bring up the movie The Matrix, and how we are all programmed like Neo, and that I am not even the real person writing this.

Simulation, that is the word. They will tell you this is a simulation, like a video game.

All questions of our reality will be brought up, by philosophers, to physicists, to priests, but none of them will confront our unusual exit from life.

We really should be asking if what makes us want to escape a life that has such a small duration anyway.

What is it about this place, this world, this life, that we don't know, or do know that makes us lean towards the side of accepting an exit from our world?

Clearly, there isn't enough here for us to want to live or stay even if we wanted to.

Lover's Confession

Look, I don't know what I'm doing here.

I may be dreaming.

This all may be fake, and I could be in some fantasy world of another creature.

After all of that, when I die, when they bury me six feet deep, and my soul departs from my body, I may find out that I don't belong in heaven.

Those angels are too good for guys like me who curse and miss church every Sunday.

And hell may not want anything to do with me either.

For I am not evil enough for them.

I may come back like a squirrel after I die because I failed to become enlightened and did not reach Nirvana.

Maybe this, all of this, has no meaning.

Maybe I'm just here, and so are you.

And what I'm feeling is not love and the passion of my heart that declares all who are against our happiness an enemy is phony.

The nervousness I felt when I first saw you, the feeling of tranquility you give me each time we meet.

All is fake.

For love is only a figment of my lost mind, a lie, a scandal, not to be believed or trusted.

I may not exist.

You may not exist.

Life may not have any purpose.

There is a distinct possibility that when I get to the end of this, there is nothing for me.

No good, no bad, no God, no Satan, nothing.

I can't stand the reality of the confusion of my existence.

I have read the great philosophers,

I know of the great writer's stories and quotes.

And I learned the great thinkers take on life.

And I have come to realize I will never know life's answers.

But I have learned that there is one thing that can overcome my fear of my understanding.

My love for you.

How I feel about you makes everything else worth it.

I don't mind if this is a simulation, or has no meaning, or that we could be living on a turtle.

Because if I can get to the end of whatever this is, and have you by my side, then I don't need to know the truth.

For the only truth, I'll ever need is right here.

My love for you.

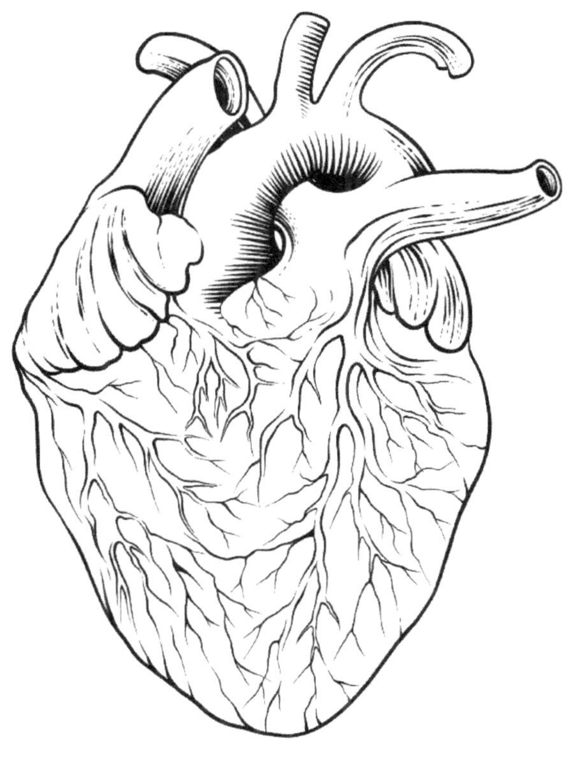

Being Nice

Don't be afraid of being nice.

Of opening the doors for others.

Of giving your hand to a stranger.

When they ask you "Who do you side with?", do not be afraid to say that you choose goodness and selflessness.

You don't value the dollar, like many others, but the integrity of a man.

You give to others.

Whether they are a black single mother or a middle-class father of three.

Kindness sees no nationality, race, or age.

You try to do right when you can.

You are polite when you meet people, courteous to strangers and show respect to all you know.

Find strength in that you have a good heart and soul.

That you feel pain when you are hurt and bleeding.

That there is a part of you, who feels something must be done when there is badness around.

Someone must feed that starving child.

Someone must defend that weak citizen.

Someone must be good in this world.

Society will tell you that kindness is not admirable.

Be tough and show you can knock someone out, then have them knock you down and get back up unmoved by the damage.

But not nice.

Be smart and invent machines that make our life easier or write words that inspire us all.

But not nice.

Be funny and bring a smile to all of our faces with a silly joke or witty remark.

But not nice.

Do not be nice, for what is there for you to gain from it?

Look at all around us and ask if kindness is needed.

We live in a world full of liars who fabricate anything
to get their way,

Rapists and killers lurk like monsters of the night
ready to prey on their next victim.

Crooks, blue and white, take what isn't theirs from
any sucker that comes by.

Corrupt leaders take bribes from gangsters and thugs
instead of fighting the problem; they become it,
allowing the culture to become desensitized to
dishonest leaders.

Dealers give out drugs to further hurt anyone willing
to pay on every street corner, church, or city center.

Or just the jackasses of everyday life who are hard to
deal with because they are mean to you.

They know no crime, and never will, but they know no
kindness either.

For their mind is smart enough to divert their
heartlessness from being caught.

If you were to choose though, you'd send them to jail,
along with the others, regardless of the lack of
evidence.

Their poor character is the fingerprints on the gun
they never shot.

There are bad people in this world, who make this a bad place to live.

Their acts bring destruction, hate, and nervousness to the world.

They make us shake our heads at mankind's fault, discouraged at the barbaric acts.

These people convince us that the Devil is not only real, but doing quite well for himself, in various counties, cities, and constructs in our world.

You are not one of those people.

Be proud of that.

You are the one who calms the rocking ship in the storm when the crew has lost hope, when the team is not playing well you are the one who silences the crowd.

Everything is going wrong!

Nothing! Nothing went right so far!

Why should we relax!

Because you are here.

Your goodness and compassion will help the situation.

Don't ever be ashamed of being nice, no matter what they tell you.

There are not enough in the world who take pride in such a thing.

Dear Future Writer

I don't know you and I never will.

You are not a part of my current world.

I'm sure historians and teachers of your day can better explain this than me.

You may know of me and my work.

You may not.

See, you are what I would call as someone in the future.

Whenever that is.

I'm in the past to you.

These original words may not be in the language you currently speak.

In fact, most of my words may be outdated to you and your contemporaries.

And you may need notes to comprehend what I'm writing now.

So what do I say to you?

The future writer who I will never meet?

Is there anything that I can say that can help you?

Or are my observations even obsolete?

Looking Out At Sea For Truman Or Columbus

I stood at the edge of the beach with the sand at my feet.

Close enough to be by the water but not in it.

At the part of the beach where no one goes.

Lifeguards, in their red uniforms and tan lines, don't guard the area.

No swimmers or surfers go by the water.

There are only beachgoers passing by aware of the lack of supervision.

Once you enter the water, you are on your own.

Lifeguards will not blow their whistles when they see you are out too far.

They won't jump from their seats and run along the sand and dive recklessly in the water when they see you drowning.

Go out and swim as far as you want.

Go to China, or whatever country you feel is so far away that the only way to get there is by extending passed safety lines at the beach.

Just try not to drown.

Resuscitation is a two-person job.

You are alone here, besides those strangers walking by.

Perhaps you'll see an older couple burnt like fried chicken with their limited beach supplies sitting and reading the newspaper.

If you are lucky, you will see a topless woman walk by and can enjoy the view.

Or unlucky, depending on the woman.

This is the part of the beach where the real beach resides.

Where nature takes over, and colorful umbrellas that must be taken down when it is windy, loud radios that play too many commercials, and icy coolers with food and soda are scarce.

The seagulls are out in a crowd near the back, away from the water being the annoying creature they always are, that God intended them to be.

Those white feathered birds always seem to have an issue on their feeble minds.

Like if they were human, they would come up to you and start something.

"You got a problem?"

Even though you only want them to leave you alone and not eat your food.

All around is sand and water for me to take in.

Depending on the day, the water, which I avoid going in, may be hot or cold.

And the sand is like that too.

Almost like nature is reminding me who makes the rules around here.

Sure I may have my phone that can connect me to another person on the other side of the world.

I can lie a human on a bed and save their life by replacing one of their organs.

I can write an hour-long symphony that will be heard by millions across the world.

I can even lie a human on a bed while listening to a symphony and create life.

The same life that inhabits the beach.

I can make a volleyball player, tan lounger, and a book reader.

I can do many things in this world.

My brain and soul gives me capabilities uncommon for mammals.

But for now, as my feet sink into the sand and my face feels the coolness of the wind, I am only a guest in the house of nature.

A scene only to be experienced in person.

My words do not do it justice, for you to understand the feeling of being in nature, not greater than it.

Sometimes as I stare into the vast ocean, I think of the iconic movie scene from *The Truman Show* where the main character travels by his boat so far out to see that he hits the wall of the studio he lives in.

The whole thing was just a set.

The sky, the sand, the pizza.

He had been living in a fake television production the whole time.

The sky of rainbows and clouds and sunshine is not the sky, but a painting of the sky.

What a feeling that would be for me to experience?

To get to the end of our world, if that even is such a thing.

How would I react?

Would I break the wall down as if I was in Berlin in the '90s?

Could I or anyone succeed in such a task?

I have a hard time opening bottles, surely the wall at the end of the world is stronger than that.

Would I "leave" the show, winking at the creator as I utter my famous catchphrase?

Or would I go back to the show, hopeless in my spiritual endeavor for my life's purpose?

The gust of summer wind, the flow of the water and the silence of the beach make me think of stuff like that.

Today though, I did not think of the boundaries of a wall, but of Christopher Columbus.

It is human nature to connect with each other.

I post poems so that strangers can read them and then I see if any of them like them later on.

We need each other.

For love of our bodies and souls, for support when we succeed and when we lose, and sometimes just for fun, to make this life a little more enjoyable.

Sometimes you don't want to hear about paying bills on time, or corrupt politicians still in office, but you want to lay back with a beer and have some laughs with your friends, as you all joke about how crazy this all is.

One of our instincts is to find others like us, to connect with others.

Yet no one looked out at sea and thought of that idea until when did the Italian travel again?

(Columbus was Italian but was employed by the Spanish, I don't know why I remember that)

What year did he discover America?

What is that rhyme that I learned in school about him that was a quick cheat to remember his accomplishment of discovering the new world?

In 1492, Columbus sailed the ocean blue.

That was the first time anyone thought of reaching out via water.

Water which was up till then, and arguably still is the most useful transportation.

Water, the element that is in me more than any other.

Water, the same thing that Thales of Miletus, one of the first philosophers ever, deduced everything was made of,

Which only makes sense to any monist out there.

Water is something from which everything can be formed, essential to life, capable of motion and change, so obviously everything is made of it.

Water, what most of our planet is composed of

Water, the element most experts agree is needed to start civilization.

Nobody looked at that water, not even Thales and thought that maybe there was someone on the other side.

That seems strange and against how we naturally are as a species.

I looked at the tranquil scenery resolved in the resolutions I will never have.

Then again I am standing at the edge of the water as an old white chested man and his wife sit together, and a nude woman walks by, so who knows?

The Mistake Book

I have a confession to make before my soul departs this world, and I am not heard of ever again.

Before I am no more, I must tell you something.

So please come closer.

A little closer.

A little closer.

Do you want me to tell you or not?

What do you want me to yell it to you?

Okay, okay, close enough.

I have a confession to tell you.

One that I have meant to for a while.

This thought has taken years off of my life.

I scream in my sleep when I dream of this disaster.

Not a day goes by that I don't regret it.

I…

I…

I…

I'm sorry for…

For…

That one book.

It was a mistake.

I should have been better with it.

I normally am quite diligent and deliberate with my books.

I rushed that one.

That's what it was.

I didn't take my time like I usually do, and my work suffered from it.

Oh…

What book am I talking about?

What does that mean?

Don't shrug your shoulders like that!

All of …

What?!

Oh, now you are just being a dick.

Get the hell out!

Forget I mentioned anything.

That's the last time I confess anything to you.

So Political

Why do these words need to be so political?

As if I am running for office.

Perhaps I can give out a sticker with these words.

You voted, be proud.

Granted every election there is a scandal on that validation process, but hell yeah, you voted.

Apparently saying the word God is offensive and mistaking someone as a man is rude

Nothing can avoid political scrutiny.

Even pointless, harmless poetry.

Damn.

Can't these words be just words?

No?

Did you ever think that giving this profound meaning is more a reflection on you than any true meaning here?

You want me to bring up controversy somehow.

Maybe race, or religion.

What else is a topic that is used by the media to push an angle?

Wow, I can name anything for the answer to that question.

I'm not doing that.

I'm not apart of that game.

I want these words not to push an agenda.

Which of course, some will interpret as an agenda in it of itself.

Non-political is still political, right?

I want these to reflect the creativity I express to convey a story and character for the reader to feel a connection with and love while learning of themselves and the world.

Or you know, something like that.

Having said all that, I do not agree with who you voted for this year.

Not About A Whale

You know that *Moby Dick* is a metaphor, right?

It is not about a real whale, but it is an analogy of man's greed for power.

The whale could also be seen as a symbol for God and man's everlasting search for the all-powerful being.

Do you know that Maya Angelou wasn't talking about an actual bird?

It was only a metaphor.

Like when Hamlet says to be or not to be, he is talking about suicide.

You know that, right?

These works seem to be over your head, yet you are quick to speak out against them.

You claim that you don't like these works.

That they never spoke to you.

Works that evidently speak to everyone but you.

Let me ask you this; how do you know that they didn't speak to you if you never read them?

If you are reading *Moby Dick* and think it is not relevant because you never saw a whale, then you are only showing how ignorant you are.

Stories don't need to take place in our universe to be loved.

How many of us have ever gone back home to our billion dollar mansion and then put on a robotic suit and go around and beat up criminals??

Not many.

Yet we all love Batman.

How many of us have gone off to another planet to get trained to use energy all around us with a light sword before we have to go and fight our father to save our friends and the galaxy?

No one.

We all love *Star Wars* though.

According to you, we should only like works if they are written about our neighborhood.

Because we don't need to be rich or a great fighter to like the character and the stories.

Just like you don't need to see a whale to like *Moby Dick*.

That Time

I'd like to go back to a simpler time,

A time I can't remember, but know well.

When I was young enough to enjoy all of this.

Before my sarcasm and wit covered up my inner wounds created by personal struggle and societal repression.

Before I learned of rules to follow, how to obey the rules, how to break the rules, and the institutions that enforce them.

There was just a boy there.

An innocent boy happy with who he was.

He didn't know much, and he didn't want to.

He never worried about paying off the finances he is in debt to, or learning of new ways to create funds for himself, or of the uncertain future, or his death.

Life was to be lived, not learned, or written off.

That boy is somewhere in this world.

I don't know where he is.

I see images from my youth of me with family and friends, and I am sure that is me in the frame.

Yet, the man I am today is not in the picture.

I'm not sure when the boy left.

Whether it was during the confusion of adolescence filled with hormones and immature jokes or the stress of adulthood with demanding managers and clock in times, or perhaps earlier.

Somewhere, sometime, he left.

He never said goodbye.

He never let me know he was leaving.

He didn't even leave a note.

One day I woke up and realized that he was not there.

What used to make me happy, makes me sad.

What used to make me laugh, makes me confused.

As my mind grew to become an adult, who knew of much, it also gained knowledge of the evils in the world, and the unanswerable questions we all have.

Once you grow up and see the world, you can't go back, even if you wanted to.

I think what scares me the most is that there are no other steps after this.

I am an adult.

I am as good as I'll ever be, at this moment.

There are no more tests to take for that degree, or schoolwork in that class to get ahead, only the obstacles that life gives me.

Somehow that joy I had as a kid is now filled with doubt, and I don't know if I can replace it.

There is no growing up anymore.

I have grown up.

Whatever I have not learned, can't be learned.

Whatever I have not done, will not be done by me.

Mistakes and errors are no longer caused by my youthful ignorance.

I have to live a life that is expected of an adult, even if my happiness is jeopardized.

I am going downhill in my life until I get to the bottom where all that meets me is a tombstone that marks the death of myself.

Although the real me may have died a long time ago.

Going Back

You can't go back to the good old days.

When you were truly happy, and before life got in the way.

Back when you had a blissful feeling in your soul that made you approach each day with a happy smile.

You can't go back to that.

To the pond with your first love in her cute dress, or to the party of your best friend's, or your grandparent's house where the family would play cards.

Wherever that place is for you, it is no more.

For me, it is a back lot of a school I attended as a kid, where we would play kickball.

We couldn't play basketball on the blacktop marked with the bases because the backboards were broken.

All the kids would try to hit the ball to the third base side, past the left fielder, (or two or three of them if there were a lot of us) because there was a large lot of grass that led to the park that kept going, and you would be guaranteed a home run.

As opposed to right field which was the school and center field which was the parking lot.

We used to make such a big deal out of the one kid who could hit the ball into the parking lot.

Each kid would celebrate when it happened, even the opposing pitcher.

Like it was some great accomplishment on our part.

Now when I drive by the school, I don't know how a lot so small could fit so many kids.

I see it as an adult, which means I see it with less innocence and more analysis.

The backboards are fixed, and if I saw a kid hit a ball into the parking lot, I wouldn't be happy and jump up and down, but thankful that the ball didn't hit my car.

The place is the same as I knew.

If I ask for directions to it, I'll receive the same location I went to as a kid.

But if I asked a stranger for the place I knew as a kid, then I would be told that it was knocked down years ago.

"Adulthood came in and took it over." The stranger would say.

"They are okay. They set up a nice office where they file papers."

They'd continue as if trying to convince me it was the right move.

"Old lot was worn down anyway."

"If you could kick the ball by the left fielder, it was an automatic home run."

I'd say as if the stranger understood me.

Adults seem to miss things kids always see.

No matter how much you think of those days.

No matter how much you dream of them.

They are gone.

And that is how it will be from now on.

Laugh about it.

Cry about it.

Forget about it.

Tell stories of it with your friends.

Take out old photos from that time.

(I can't believe you were that young either.)

Whatever you do, you can't go back.

I'm sorry, but you can't.

Don't bother trying to, you'll only waste your time.

Be happy that the ball didn't hit your car and move on.

SCHOOL

The Question

There is a question you will have in your life you need to know.

At least I expect that to be the case.

If you are a human being with any sensible brain and enough rationale you will demand that this question is answered.

I suppose that if you are a naïve, thoughtless person who never knows of critical ideas, or of pondering, then you will not have this problem.

The catch is that someone lays out the answer to your question, for you simply don't know.

You have heard of and know of the other examples of this unique situation where the lesson is told to you, like that of a child.

Your parents explain, probably awkwardly, for you and them, sex and reproduction and you must sit and bare the embarrassment that you were created because your mom and dad had sex.

And it turns out that everyone has sex; it is not even that big of an accomplishment on their end.

Schools are a place where people who had sex send their results of that orgasm.

You learn that a kiss is not only a kiss and those music lyrics have another meaning, which could explain why some people gave you strange looks when you sang those words aloud as a kid.

You had to be told of this because your feeble mind could not grasp it by learning it on your own.

Then there is the always uplifting topic of death.

Like sex, it is everywhere, but unlike sex, we don't like it.

In fact, we try to avoid death as much as we can.

But still, an older person, probably your parents too, have to explain that people die.

We can't live forever.

Even if you all loved your grandpa, he had to die.

Why?

Because that is how life is.

And you must accept the harsh reality of this world.

Everyone you ever met will die one day, as your ancestors did before you.

And so will you.

No matter what you do, this day will come.

Maybe you will die heroically, like in a battle against an enemy that is to be taken down similar to a legend like that of Beowulf,

Or maybe you'll die in a forgetful manner, more suited to a sitcom than real life, like choking on a hot dog in your kitchen.

Both situations had you guided towards the proper answer, because, truth to be told, you didn't know it at the time.

Like a confused kid on a test, you needed someone over your shoulder to point out the right answer.

Then there is a third one that is arguably the most important of the three.

It is another time in your life you expect a person who knows more than you to give you a hand, a whisper in your ear, a demonstration.

But this time, this question may not get answered.

What is all of this?

Who am I?

What am I doing here?

Do you know?

Does anybody know?

Okay, I lied, it isn't one question exactly.

It is more like a bunch of questions around a certain topic.

I hate to say it, but no one knows what you are doing here, or what I am doing here, or what any of us are doing here.

No one I have met in this world knows of my purpose here or their purpose.

I simply am, as I will be, and live life.

Will I ever be told of my questions?

Maybe when I get to the end, God can sit me down, and explain my life to me in a way I understand, so that I can reach an epiphany of my actions.

Which if I am fair, seems rather cruel to have me live an ignorant life of a hundred years, only for me to learn of the lessons after it.

That is like taking a test and learning the answers only afterward, at a time when your knowledge of them does nothing to further your education.

Some study guide would help.

Life has no study guide though.

You will be told an answer to basically everything in this world.

Anything you can think of, has an answer, that society can be certain.

But the most important question you have is not answered by anyone.

It can only be answered by you.

Early Afternoon

What do you do early in the afternoon,

When all the work is done,

And your tasks are through?

I know, I can't believe it's true.

There is nothing here for us to do.

Nothing is even due.

Not true!

Not true!

I know there is work to do.

Maybe I can help with the new issue.

No?

Doesn't anybody have a clue?

Sue?

Lou?

Andrew Baloo?

Anyone of you?

What?

I'm too eager, too soon?

Leave for the afternoon.

And do whatever I do?

Oh, yeah, that works too.

The Words of Mr. 500

Let me make myself real clear to you

If you try to take away my gun, I'll shoot you.

See you think I'm holding this out of hate, out of madness, and you're wrong.

The last thing I want to do with my gun is to kill someone with it.

I hold onto this because of love, not hate.

I love myself enough to give myself a chance against those who hate me and want me dead, those who you assume I am because I have a gun in my possession.

Don't you think I ought to give myself a chance of survival in case I get attacked?

We are fighting the same fight, one against the foe of evil, of those who wish to wreak havoc upon this Earth for no reason at all,

But that is where we differ my friend,

You want us all to hold hands and sing koom-ba-yah and love each other.

No guns for everyone to make the world a better place.

That sounds good, but we both know is not how this crazy world functions.

Unfortunately, some don't want peace and harmony.

Some want violence and mayhem.

And Mr. 500 here is my answer to them.

And you cannot win a fight without a weapon.

I also have my family, who mean everything to me, and that woman right over there is the love of my life, and I'd do anything for her.

I have two young ones upstairs who are my greatest accomplishments in this life.

Not a day goes by that I don't pray for them and try to love them with all my heart.

If you try to hurt them, then I gonna try to hurt you.

Now you want me to give you my gun, despite no threats from me.

I do not know you, nor wish you harm.

But when you take away my gun, well that is a problem.

See this protects them, and me.

And I like them more than you.

I'm an honest, kind man to most but when you get in my way like this without a threat from me, I can change rather quickly, out of love, not hate.

Here you go.

Here's your threat.

Don't think I won't hesitate to put one in your chest if you try to take this away from me.

Cause you forget one thing about my friend here, Mr. 500.

He doesn't have a bias when he talks, like you and me.

No Paper

How the hell do I not have paper?

What the hell!

I am a writer for Christ's sake!

My job is to write on paper!

And I have no paper?

None?

Anywhere?

Not in the printer, or on another desk, or underneath the chair.

I don't even have a notebook to jot a few words down.

Really?

Maybe I am wrong.

I'll look again.

No.

There is still no paper in the printer.

I could have sworn when I looked away for a second that the paper would magically appear.

I'm an idiot, and I have no paper, which is always a great way to start writing.

That is my new way of writing, without paper.

Pretty soon, I'll get rid of my pens too, and I'll have no way to write down my words.

Jesus Christ. I had a great story idea too.

It was about a town that was on drugs.

Each character was addicted to a drug and then that would a ….

Well, it would mean something, I'm sure.

And then the characters would, well, talk and interact I guess.

I didn't really think much about the plot.

Something would happen in the story that reflects the theme of our overuse of drugs in modern culture.

Look, it made sense to me when I was thinking about it.

It was just a basic idea to get going.

And I'D BE ABLE TO WRITE IT DOWN IF I HAD SOME PAPER!

God, I am such an idiot sometimes.

An Irishman's Fate

I'm stricken to an Irishman's fate of no glory and no honor in my life.

Nothing but that of a forgotten footnote of our existence.

Seen as inbreeds, as outcasts, yet never proud of our degenerative culture.

The world sheds no tears for the Irish.

There are no museums teaching of our past.

Schools do not mention our history to the students.

Nothing is heard of them.

As if they are not that important at all.

The most we talk of them is when the world mocks them as we all get drunk.

That is all an Irishman is to the world.

Other groups can be proud of who they are, where they came from, how they got here.

The struggle of their people, but not the Irish.

The greatest struggle of an Irishman is with himself,
for only he can come to grips of the reality,

The world does not care for you.

If you sin, if you sing.

If you win, if you write.

No matter what you do, it doesn't matter to anyone.

An Irishman being in a room, and not being in a room,
is not all that different.

No matter where these words go, whether to the
footsteps of the king or the bookshelves of fans.

I will be nothing more than an Irishman to anyone.

Part of a group of people the world is not proud to
know.

Have To

I have to do this.

I have to succeed with this.

I have no choice.

It's not because I love to do it, or some sort of passion on my end.

It's because I am not going to be working here for the rest of my life.

I am not going to waste away in a warehouse being another worker who picks up boxes all day long.

No.

I won't become another name on the list of people that could have been something in this world.

I know too many of those people.

Who killed their dreams because they had to because the world told them to.

And they are left to be resolved in the current restraints of our society, happy but not doing what they love.

"He was good." They all say of those on the list.

As they begin to contemplate why the individual didn't make it.

Was it drugs?

Did some tragedy happen in the family that took too much of their time?

They all end with the same thought.

"For a guy so talented he didn't do much with it."

No.

I refuse to let that happen to me.

This isn't about winning at this point.

It's not about writing great material or even getting better.

It's about not having my life past me by and becoming a nobody.

The only thing that matters is figuring out a way to get out of this place.

If I stay here too long, I may never leave.

Want To Believe

I want to believe that my heroes are fighting the good fight.

That they stand for goodness and all noble qualities.

That they are trying to make the world a better place.

And they did not succumb to the ever-growing evil to achieve fame.

That hard work and some luck helped them, more than anything else.

I want to believe that they are true in their ways.

I do.

But after all that I learned of the crazy world,

How can I?

How can I not be suspicious of anyone popular after learning of some who do bad to get there?

The pool is all green, yet you expect me to think that you are clean when you get out?

At a closed restaurant, you are the one they serve?

On a block full of robbers, you are the one cop?

How can I believe that?

All heroes become questionable at one point or another.

Society takes away their hero badge and rejects them.

Bad!

Bad!

Bad! Bad! Bad! Bad! Bad!

And when this happens, you have to decide who do you believe?

Your hero, who until that time was not wrong in your eyes.

And who even taught you a few valuable lessons you keep till this day.

Or the evidence that proves otherwise.

That says they are not the hero you knew and loved.

After that, you can then wonder how you fell for it in the first place.

A Cursed Man

I'm accused of being a man of no man in this world.

Shallow, thick darkness fills my veins for the weak one who left me on my own.

I am not you!

We do not share the same blood, same name, same eyes.

How dare you say such a thing!

I am my own man, and I built my path through this life with no help from you.

But does a man's life not include his past?

And that makes you a part of me.

You, the fool.

You, the coward.

You, the weak.

You, who thought it was best to leave than stay.

The worst thing a man can do is abandon his child as if it is not his own.

For that is when a man is needed most in life.

Not for war, or politics, but nurture of the youth.

You are a part of me, and there is nothing I can do about that.

I am forever ashamed to know you.

I hate you, because in the end, cruelly, you win.

If I stay with you, I learn of what a pathetic loser you are, a vagabond, a drifter, with no purpose or goal.

And if I leave you, then I do not get to know the man who is my father.

For this, I am a cursed man.

String Of Lies

One day we will look back on all of this, on all the news, on all the stories, on all the gossip, and learn of what a fraud it really was.

They lied.

It is really that simple.

They chose a narrative, an angle, that had no factual evidence.

They lied right in front of us.

There is no boogeyman hiding in our closet, no unknown threat we don't understand, no hidden enemy we can't detect.

There, you see that he is not telling the truth and we believed him.

It was an elaborate lie.

And they were clever in how they did it.

But a lie of a right man is the same as a lie of a wrong man.

It is still a lie.

And we bought it.

Since then, we fought over it.

We changed over it.

We even cried over it.

And it was all a lie.

A con of a thief.

A trick of a magician.

A riddle of a jester.

If there is anything we can learn from this, it is to not take anyone with authority as truthful.

We must learn to question anyone who demands respect.

Who stands up and claims they have something important to say.

If we don't, then this string of lies will happen again, until all we know are lies.

No Hope

I want to ask an obscure question that is not right for this book.

How do you control people?

Is there some diabolical code to put into a computer?

Is there a club that specializes in that stuff?

Here is what you do; take away their hope.

Make people think they don't matter.

They have no opinions, other than the ones you give them, of course.

And those opinions are only in favor of you.

Not for an objective, rational outlook, but a blinded shallow one.

Tell people that their voice, their vote is meaningless.

That way they don't do anything about it.

"Why should I vote? It is not like it matters anyway?"

How many times have we all heard this before?

People stay clear of anything they can do, and why not, since what they do is pointless anyway, right?

One man can't change the world.

Hard work and honesty are not agreeable traits for one to have.

And your vote does not matter.

You don't matter if you are not in agreement with what they say.

If you want to be ambitious, tell the people there is nothing else but here, the present.

This life, this existence.

Don't look forward to the future, for that it too far away and no one can prepare for it.

The past is irrelevant and a waste of time.

Those of historical eras lived a vastly different lifestyle, so they shouldn't be learned about anyway.

All that matters is now.

This is the most important thing ever.

What you are doing is the most relevant event in the history of the world.

And what is now?

A desperate, pathetic world where you don't matter and have no real impact.

That is what they will tell you.

Beware of the man who does not seek truth and is suspicious of goodness.

Of those who rip down the masses, rather than build them up.

No matter how much they tell you this message, don't believe it.

Remember that the enemy is fine with you believing you can't win.

The Year 1318

I know history pretty well.

So much that when I receive a receipt, I guess what happened in that year.

The amount for my purchase was $13.18

1318.

What happened in 1318?

Did anything happen in that year?

Of course, something did.

(Is that not the case for all years?)

The Plague!

The Black Death.

The worst epidemic in the history of the world, killing 1/3 of the population of Europe.

Rats caused it.

The rodents spread from town to town spreading the disease.

The other bad epidemic was the Spanish Flu, but that was much later.

That killed more people, something like 120 million if I'm correct, but it didn't have as high of a percentage.

I guess it depends on how you judge an epidemic, for which you consider to be the worse of the two.

The Plague lasted a few years.

Can I name anyone from that year?

Someone, you know, important.

That did something, that would be an answer to a question on a test in school or Jeopardy.

We have documents of people who lived during that time.

Court cases, original manuscripts, signatures.

People existed in that year.

I'm not making that up.

Holy crap.

How can I not name one individual from that year?

Were there no corrupt rulers who abused their power with slick lies to the gullible masses and powerful weapons against their enemies causing war across nations, in the name of controlled peace?

No commoners who led a revolution claiming that their lives matter, despite the rules of the day that would say otherwise.

Were there no explorers who discovered new rich lands and congregated with royals over trades and economy?

Boy, I'm an idiot.

And you know that there was someone during 1318 who thought the year was the most important year ever.

And others may have agreed with that person.

Like they were apart of a great dramatic war with heroes and villains and lessons for future generations, or something that when you are in it, you are convinced your legacy is sealed and fate stamped and matches that of Jesus.

Only for no reason at all, it's not important to future generations.

That war wasn't *the* war.

That book wasn't *the* book.

That leader wasn't *the* leader.

Sorry, for a second, while it was going on, I would have put money on it too.

Am I in the year 1318? (metaphorically speaking)

Will one day someone in the future says the same thing I just said about 1318?

2018?

Nothing happened during that year.

You don't have to even know about it.

It is a forgetful footnote in history.

Bypass it to save time.

Throw it away with the latest fad.

Erase it faster than an elder's mind does a memory.

The only thing you have to know about 2018 is that you don't need to know it at all.

Nothing happened in 2018, only my life.

Those are overrated anyway.

RECEIPT
TOTAL

Enough Tears

If I cry enough and pour out my soul and heart to the coolness of my pillow, will you come back?

If I sit here, alone in my empty room, and never stop crying, never stop the pain, will you come back to me?

Will my cries be heard from across town and where you will run over to save me?

Like a hero from an old time love story.

Stop dear. Do not cry.

For I am here to love you for the rest of your days.

And what is heartache to a loving heart?

What if I cry a river's worth of tears as big as the Nile and Mississippi combined?

What if I cry an ocean?

Or all of the world?

If I cry all of the world's water, all that keeps us alive, will you come back?

Is there any amount of tears, any at all, that will make you come back?

Please.

Please don't answer that.

As I drown in my own tears caused by the heartbreak, let me believe that there is some way you will come back.

Even though we both know the answer to that.

Thinking Of You

I thought of you, in all your captivating beauty when I wrote this down.

I can't have you in my life, so these words will have to do.

Like all things, our time together will become a memory, one that I may question ever occurred.

Was my time with you a dream, a fantasy?

Did I accidentally misremember my life?

Was, it that long ago?

And all I will have then, will not be you, but this poem.

I write these words of love not for you, for we both know you don't need them.

But for me, and that fateful unfortunate event, when I forget how much I cared, how much you meant to me, how much I loved you.

When life acts as a wicked thief and takes so much from my mind that I barely remember my name.

This is proof that I loved you when I met you, and I love you as I write this, and I will always love you.

Even when you fade from my mind.

Love is not limited to the mind but is more than emotion, more than the heart.

You gave me the love that was more than love.

But in case that love is gone from me.

And destiny gives me a cruel hand, I will have this poem, so I know my heart was, is, and forever will be yours.

History's Outlook

I hope, like the heart of a broken Christian in church during mass, when I am long gone from this Earth,

When the world forgets my name, my acts, and my words, that am I correct with my outlook on this world.

(To be forgotten is almost inevitable if you ask me.

Each man's legacy is a clock and is only a matter of time before he is passed over and no longer relevant to the current world he once served.

A world that harbors the same species he once knew and loved.)

In my dreams, when I am away in my mind, I wish to see my name to continue long after my corpse hits the ground,

But that is not reality, and why it is a dream.

I hope that, despite my shortcomings of myself and personal life, and my lack of knowledge due to my current period, I was right in my life's choices.

That I can look back on all I did, in my short life here, which is if I am lucky is one hundred years, and if I am like so many wordsmiths not even fifty, and know that I chose wisely in my life's decisions.

That I was on the right side of history,

No. Not history, history is man's works.

Our retelling of the past we want to remember and the present we wish to see.

History is much of fabrication as the very fiction I write.

I want to be on the right side of them… oh, what do you call it exactly?

Whatever it is, I want to be right in my stand.

Good Ol' Chuck

Meet Chuck.

He's fine fella, good ol' Chuck.

Or as some call him Buck.

(Although I don't know why)

Perhaps he is a good hunter.

Or maybe people like that it rhymes with his real name.

Others are known to call him a real dumb fu...

But we won't get into that.

As Chuck or Buck, (whichever you prefer) always says

"Sometimes you can't give a fu..."

"Don't ever say this to anyone." He told me.

"Or else they'll think you're a real dumb fu..."

Inadequate

Two men, already tired of the day, stood in the aisle searching for the items they needed to complete their job.

"Look at this.

This is a mess.

Nothing is in the right place.

I swear to God,

Every time.

Every time, we are here."

"Ah, don't let it bother you."

The man, not searching, stopped his colleague's rant.

"This place is....

Well, you know."

Another man walked by the two and put back a few items he did not want to buy.

"Inadequate is the word I believe, you are looking for."

They stared perplexed at the stranger.

"You think the guy who works here sucks."

"He does.

Look at this.

It's as if no one works here."

The stranger walked down the aisle to attend to some items that he saw.

After not much more deliberation, the two men left the aisle leaving a mess of the unpurchased items.

The worker headed back down the aisle to put back the various items.

The Collins Conundrum

Poetry with all its flaws, (like alcohol at a family reunion, there is a lot to go around)

And its beauty, which believes it or not, does exist.

Needs men like Billy Collins who are unconventional in their style.

Who doesn't write like the "other" poems?

Thy lord is upon my head and guides it unto a light that only it knows.

Without the light of the Lord, I have no light at all.

I am darkened by a dark world, filled with nothing but the darkness.

My head is empty, basin and deserted, without thy Lord.

Comfort me, Lord, with your light and glory.

I get it; you like God.

Or those other poems that are so confusing.

Thou art thy rose in a garden of plants that seeks shelter from the pervading sun as it shines the wholesome energy upon thy cheeks.

Love me unconditionally as our only condition.

Wasps may sting, bees may buzz, and clouds will rise, but my love for you in all grandeur and spectacle that any man would meet Death twice, to know, is forever.

Those are so disconcerting that the reader is left asking "Did the writer know what they were doing as they wrote this?"

I bet there was some alcohol involved.

Billy gets it.

He makes poetry simple so morons like myself can understand it.

He may be on to something there too since most people are like me.

Why talk to the few intellects, when the world is full of fools?

Billy mocks the standard poetry we came to know and run from as soon as we hear it.

"Is he talking about poetry?

I gotta go. I.... I... have this thing, that stuff happens and look. I'll see you later."

Whatever excuse getting out of those damn words.

As he rips apart the status, he creates his own.

Out is in.

Left is right.

Bad is good.

And poetry is somehow still confusing.

How can a rule be an exception and standard for the other rules?

That makes no sense.

Unconventional is a convention, no matter how much we are told otherwise.

Can you be a convention while being unconventional?

Can a rich man know the struggles of a missed payment?

Does the athlete know the hardships of the obese?

What can the healthy say of the sick?

Somehow Billy Collins proves the very thing we have known all along.

We have no idea what we are reading.

I Killed My Boss

I killed my boss yesterday before the day was over.

I was tired of all of his bullshit, and his treatment towards me.

So I killed him.

The only way to rid of a problem is through the elimination of the cause.

His existence was the cause of my anger.

Without him, I won't be mad at the world.

I took the axe out of the trunk of my car and marched right into his room.

He was all alone sitting at his desk when he turned to me.

I didn't ask him how his day was, or what he was doing for the weekend.

I walked up to him, and I swung away.

And before I knew it, I was full of blood, and he was dead in the chair.

Somehow he still looked like a jackass, with the axe stuck in his chest.

Afterward, someone in the office called the cops, and I got taken in.

I didn't put up a fight or try to run.

I just hung out in the office until they arrived.

Being in the police vehicle in handcuffs for murdering a man I hated, is making me reconsider my actions.

I probably should have poisoned him.

The Search

They will search for my past.

The will scour my history.

They will go back in time if they have to.

And why?

So you believe that I'm the bad guy.

Yes. Yes.

Let us line all the corrupt, all the evil, all the wrong.

And throw my name next to them.

Have I taken money on the side?

Have I killed innocents?

Have I abused unsuspecting victims?

No, but my enemies know my fall is easiest when the public is against me.

What will they do, if they have nothing on me?

Lie.

They will all say the same clever lie.

All my enemies, who wish to have me see no more of this Earth,

Who will strip my clothes off of my corpse, and plant the gun on my side after shooting me,

They lead me to the wolves and watch on as the animals shred me to pieces.

They close the door on me as the room fills with poisonous gases.

My death is their celebration.

A lie to them is much if it means my demise.

And who are you to believe?

Me?

Who would then be presented as a criminal, not to be trusted, but boycotted.

Or them?

Who repeat those same words in your ears, until it is the only opinion you have.

He is bad.

They'll say to you.

But you may not see it.

He is bad.

They'll repeat, in case you didn't hear them the first time.

And you are starting to question my past.

He is bad.

And then you will connect dots from two different unrelated pictures of my life to see the one of me as a villain.

And it all comes clear to you, like the sky on a summer's day.

I am the bad guy.

How did you not see it before?

Despite my clean hands and good heart, I sit at the table with vagabonds and crooks, singing choruses of our robberies and tricks.

The Devil invites me over for dinner.

A reward goes for any who could kill me and drag my body out into the streets.

An extra will go to whoever brings my head.

At this time of my downfall, empathy is forgotten, like a poorly taught history lesson.

Liars, scammers, and slackers, all the good of this world, decide I deserve no forgiveness, no love, no second chance.

And those that I loved who I tried to help, and inspire, turn on me.

And wish none other than my death.

And you know what?

They may get it.

Life (What Is It Again)

Life is but a dream.

Or is it a dream within a dream?

Or is life a dream within a dream, within a dream?

How many dreams is life within?

Five, ten, twenty maybe?

What would that make this then?

A dream within a dream, within a dream.

Wow, that is quite some dream.

Did you get that?

Do you need me to repeat it?

I get the feeling that once we are within five or more dreams, we are no longer talking about life or even dreams.

Which sucks, since I'm lost for what we are talking about then.

Do I even want to ask whose dream this is?

Nevermind.

Act like I never mentioned it.

One Of Us

No matter what you do.

And all the accolades and honor the world bestows upon you.

I know only one truth of you.

If you perform miracles, that no mere mortal man can do, for all to see.

If you turn water to wine or feed thousands with only a piece of bread.

If you tame the Nemean Lion or bring us the head of the Hydra.

I don't care.

We do not care.

Save a nation from its own destruction, caused by political and social turmoil, with your great words and good actions.

Inspire the world, from the kings to the vagabonds, and all the players in between, with your words of wisdom and dramatic scenes.

Or invent a new system of mathematics that reshapes our understanding of the known world.

Do whatever.

One hundred, or zero percent.

Go all out and bleed for your people, die for your nation, struggle for your words.

Or shed no tears, no effort, no strain, of any kind and be a bum, known only to bartenders and miscreants.

Play this as you wish.

I don't care.

We do not care.

Cause no matter what you do, where you do it, and you will never be one of us.

I and everyone is in this room, will never accept you as one of our own.

No one here will ever call you brother.

Sick Bastards

"Why do you write of such grotesque disturbing unholy sights?

What is your cause for the creation of such art?"

"Because people are sick bastards.

Why do you think people still read Poe after all these years?

Because he is uplifting and inspirational?

No. It's because we like the weird,

The kooky, the crazy, the unsafe (that may kill us)

We like horror, crime, and darkness.

We enjoy tales of murder and torture and pain.

Where a man gets his head chopped, or a woman gets mutilated.

Where zombies come back from the dead, or a person is haunted.

We are attracted to evil.

To the monsters that only want to hurt us.

Like the werewolves, with their transformation and moon-howling, or Frankenstein and his bolts,

And ghosts, demons, and ghouls that stalk the night.

Things that we know we shouldn't like we like.

All that sick stuff that makes our stomach churn, our eyes look away and our soul frustrated, we want.

And the sicker, the better.

Give us more blood, more corpses, more misery.

Don't only hurt a person, show it and explain in very specific details, how it's done.

Cause we want to know it.

The woman being tied up and whipped.

The saw cutting into a person's bones.

The sound of the stalker's footsteps

Don't hold back.

Give all the evil we can handle, and then double it.

Once and a while someone creates a piece of art that reflects that side of us.

A side we know is bad, but don't mind having.

If you want to know why this is popular, do not ask me, ask yourself."

Signature For A Dead Store

As I sign this book contract for consignment, my ignorance is the true signee.

Sure, that name there is legible, but don't be fooled for that is for show.

Like a nod to a stranger walking by, only a formality to keep our fragile work in check.

I have to agree to allow to sell the book at...

...

That price?

Damn. I underestimated the price.

I thought I'd be making more from this transaction.

And they only want, how many?

Three books?

Damn. I miscalculated this one.

I disregard my faulty projections and quickly answer whatever questions the cute cashier has for me.

The hipster with her general indifference to life and torn jeans is about my age and mentions that she would read the book.

I thank her, whether she ever does so is an action I'm not worried about.

But acceptance of a compliment is better than confrontation when advancement is desired.

I'm not complaining of the price or copies since getting in a bookstore *is* getting in a bookstore.

Or so I think as I sign to what I believe is the beginning of a career as a real writer.

This is the bookstore that will start it all.

That I can go back to after a long successful career and say they discovered me first.

My book will sell out in this bookstore in no time.

Youth and ignorance are great ingredients for unreasonable expectations.

And I had plenty.

Little do I know that this bookstore will not be here in three years.

And that it has been facing financial problems for a decade.

All the books that surround me as I walk out.

The books which can only found in independent bookstores will be sold for half off to anyone who wants to buy it.

My three books will be picked up, not by a customer asking for a bestseller, but by accident, by someone who just so happened to learn that the bookstore was closing.

I don't know that.

The cashier, may not even know that.

In Line With Billy Collins

I stood in line at Barnes and Nobles with two classics I feel, I should know about if I am going to do with whole writing thing for real.

Gilgamesh, and *As You Like It*.

The most I can tell you about *Gilgamesh* is that it is an epic like *The Odyssey*.

Only it isn't.

What I mean is that it was recently discovered on some rocks, (history calls them tablets, but I know rocks when I see them) and hidden from the public.

Unlike *The Odyssey* which is still read in schools.

This *Gilgamesh* character, aside from having a name that reminds me of an intriguing Italian cuisine, was around for a much longer time than that classical piece by Homer.

Why I need to know such information before opening the pages is a question I can't answer.

Are there that many readers rejecting epics because they came after *The Odyssey*?

Or where are those readers who read a book because it came before another one?

There must be plenty of them out there, that I am not familiar with.

The other book I was clinching in my fist was *As You Like It*.

By Shakespeare.

Yeah, that Shakespeare.

The Shakespeare that your favorite movie probably took from without telling you.

Or when there is a Romeo in the room, someone is bound to say, 'Romeo where art thou Romeo.'

Or advertisers use their products as a spoof of his take on suicide.

It is not "to be or not to be," but to (whatever they are selling), or not to (whatever they are selling)

The Shakespeare that you kind of have to know if you speak English around here.

That guy.

I was holding a book by him and knew little to nothing about it.

The most I know is that it isn't *Hamlet* or *Romeo and Juliet*, which is only saying that it is not considered a timeless masterpiece that should be read long into the future.

Or maybe it is.

I could be wrong there.

Standing in front of me was an older man who looked like a famous poet I read a few times.

No, not Shakespeare.

Although it would be fun seeing him in line, I'd probably be freaked out over the sight of a dead man.

It was the American poet, Billy Collins, who any poetry fan, can see him in my style.

Yes, the one you are reading right now.

What are some of those words that critics use for him as selling points to buy his books?

Simple yet, eloquence,

Profound, yet understandable.

Stuff like that.

I've heard people say that about me too.

Which is nice, I guess.

The guy looked like him.

Or what I remembered of his appearance when I read the back author page that is a necessity in today's literature world.

(I don't know why. Don't ask me. I'm not an editor.)

It only resembled him as much as that I will tell others I met him once at a bookstore and feel confident that I wasn't telling that big of a white lie.

If I am really in a good mood, I will say how he knew of my work and was a big fan.

When I am sixty, I won't just have met him, but we spoke of what became of a classic I wrote later on.

That interaction with him sparked it all.

I was staring at pop-up letters in the stand that are supposed to be father's day gifts but seem more like a cruel joke to me when "Billy" spoke up.

"Don't ever get behind me when you're in a store, or you'll never move."

"Oh." His humor caught me off guard. "Yeah."

"I normally pick the line that goes slower, when there are two lines, that is."

There was only one line.

"It's much better when there is a self-checkout line." The "Poet Laureate" said.

"Oh yeah.

One time I was waiting on line when the person was holding everyone up was complaining about the book they were returning.

How it wasn't like how they bought it.

How they were upset with the store's workers.

The guy wasn't even buying a book and holding everyone up."

"Billy" went next.

A few moments later I hear the cashier tell him they couldn't renew his membership, but that he could still shop.

So apparently "Billy" didn't buy a book either.

For the record, I can't tell you if this personality fits the poet at all, for I have never met him.

I only know of his words, and like many common readers, do not expect to see literary greatness at a local bookstore, as I dream of a place in literature lore I neither deserve nor receive.

But I'd like to think this does.

And to think I was going to buy *The Trouble With Poetry* instead of *Gilgamesh*.

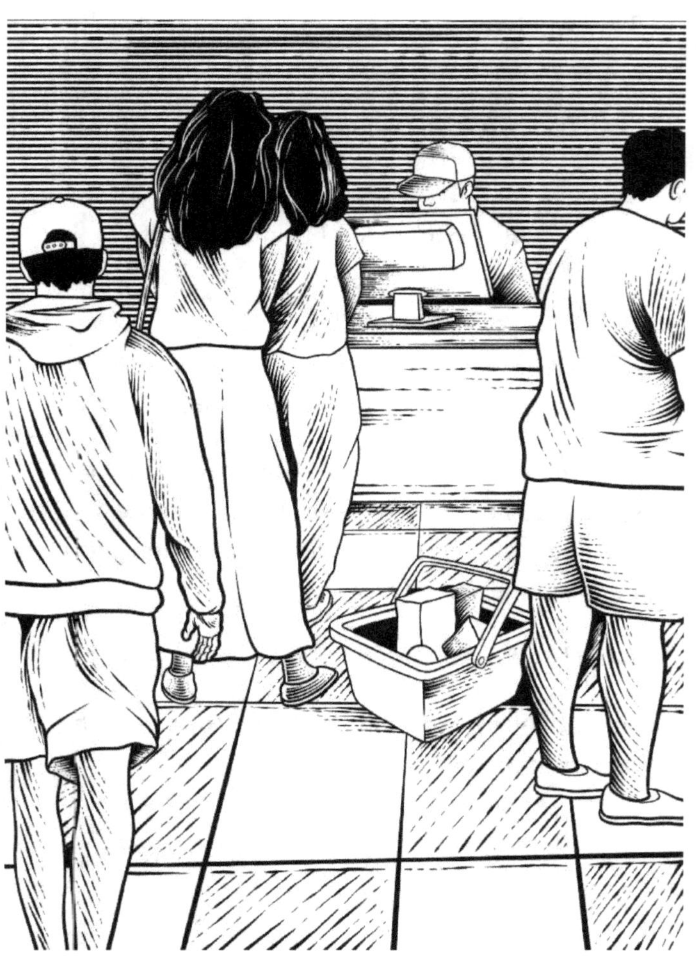

One Less At Dinner

"Kids! Dinner."

Mom called to us as we ran to the table.

"Where's Jerry?" I asked as we all sat down to eat.

"Yeah. I haven't seen him all day."

My brother stated.

In all the proper etiquette of a professional chef,
Mom sat at the head of the small table.

You call tell she was proud of the meal she put
together.

"Jerry will not be eating with us tonight.

We were all out of food.

And he gave me a problem when I asked him to go
and get me some from the market.

So I cooked him."

She said a matter of factly.

"Ha. Ha. Real funny.

Where is he?"

"I'm not sure why you are laughing.

We really are eating him."

Pretend Tears

I'm going to pretend that you loved me.

That we had something special.

That I was your Romeo and did all I could to win you over.

That we were meant to be as soon as we met.

That we had memorable times only we could remember.

That we bonded like friends, loved like lovers, and laughed like family.

That as soon as we spilled, you regretted the decision.

I'm going to pretend that you cared about me, as much as I did you.

So these tears,

These tears of restless heartache,

Tears of nerve-racking depression,

Tears of deep sadness,

Tears of all I know and am,

Can mean something.

These are the same tears a man cries because of passion, gained or lost.

That is at a funeral cause of a dead friend.

Or at a wedding because of a lover found.

Those tears that nature recognizes as my acceptance of life's journey.

That can only be accompanied by a real person.

Those tears fall my face as if I am supposed to have loved you.

But alas, I'm alone, and I shouldn't be this way.

I pretend that you loved me so that these tears can mean something.

Hide It

Two co-workers ready to leave their jobs were pushing their garbage cans to the dumpster when they were both stopped by a worker in another department.

"Do you mind moving that thing in the aisle? I don't know what it is."

One of the workers agreed and walked back alone to the area of the obstruction, as the other waited.

"What did he want?"

The waiter asked the other when he got back, and they were out of earshot anyone.

"He wanted that box out of the aisle and put back."

"But I thought we didn't sell that."

"We don't. I put it back, behind something else, out of the way."

"Works for me."

They pushed their cans towards the dumpster and avoided any more conversation when they got there.

TRASH
TRASH

Actors

I do not trust actors, with their great looks, and elaborate costumes and multiple awards show.

This is not for my disinterest in films.

For I, as much as the next person, love em.

I still get a thrill from sitting down in a theater and watching a good movie.

I do not like them since they have different motives, towards their work than an author.

They say words given to them.

Authors create the words and hope to present an opportunity for discussion from the reader.

Not to push their views, but to let the audience decide.

Actors do not seek the truth or question the world around them.

Their characters might, but they do not.

A villain with a snarl and cane going to the ends of the world to kill their opponent.

A hero who does all he can, travels the seas and foreign lands, to get back to save his family.

Or the comic foil, who mocks himself openly as being pathetic and useless to live.

A role is a role to an actor.

It is all the same.

Just a part to nail.

Nothing more.

Whether that character is good or not doesn't matter.

Actors; they say, and we accept.

Views of the progressive left, or conservative right, or moderates.

They don't care if the audience ever has to think.

This expected lack of thought from the audience makes me at odds with films, since these actors, are doing the opposite of me.

Or at least what I believe I am doing.

But who am I to say this of actors?

Have I ever been in a room of other hopefuls trying to get the part?

Do I know what it is like to deal with an abusive director who will not stop until the scene is perfect?

Have I ever stood next to an unbearable human being off the screen only to have to lie and pretend to love him or her when the camera is on?

What do I know of the movie industry?

And how dare I say such things as a writer?

A poet, whose mixed words and complex ideas somehow form to make lines that the readers, some of who are actors, read.

Excuse me for such an inappropriate gathering of statements.

I hope that actors do not judge authors as I wrongly judged them.

Authors, what do they do; but sit around all day and type up words from stories that aren't even original and then people read them, and they think they are so great.

Authors, all are pretending to be so smart because they can tell you about alliteration or hyperbole or canon.

Authors, whose biggest thrill in life is to see their names, which they most likely made up, on a book in a store.

Authors, whose being physical strain they have in their job is moving their fingers.

Authors, who even coined an excuse for when they can't write a story.

Do not criticize actors, for, without them, authors have nothing to write about.

The author may write the story, but the actor brings it to life.

Who am I kidding here?

Who am I trying to fool with this critique of actors that I wish to see in films?

Do I not pretend when I write a story?

Do I not make things up?

Do I not wish to be someone else?

Perhaps a king from a far off land, or a powerful alien from another planet?

Are we not all actors?

Could it be, we all love actors so much because they are who we all are.

We aren't seeing actors on the screen.

We see ourselves.

Remind Me Of My Soul

Remind me of who I am.

And that there is more to me than what they say of me.

More than what they want.

More than what I gave them.

Remind me that I have a soul.

That I'm fighting for the right side in all of this.

My uniform is marked black for a demon to approve but underneath is a seal only an angel can understand.

Remind me that I am really good on the inside.

And the love of God fuels my inspiration, nothing else.

And I only pretended to dance with the Devil.

Yes, that is all it was.

A dance, a fling.

A subtle glare across an empty room.

For I learned early on, that there is no room for a Christian in the land of heathens.

I still have a chance.

Please tell me, that I still have a chance.

Please.

I don't want to do this anymore.

The wardrobe of lies and deceit can no longer be worn by my criminal mind.

Tell me that I am still the good-hearted man you used to know.

Before all of this took over.

You were always more religious than me so please...

Tell me I am not lost.

That God will help me.

The symbols of blasphemy, the names of the wicked occult, all of it, was a ruse, a deception.

Not from God, but Satan.

For I played the Devil's game only to get by.

I drank the wine of the cold-hearted leader.

I passed the tests to belong to the powerful corrupt.

I attended the parties

Not because I don't have faith.

But as an undercover.

To show God of his enemy's ways.

Remind me, after all the shame I brought, all the hate I grew, all the wrong I produced, that I still have a soul.

Please, I need to know that Jesus will still give me a chance.

Hating The Boss

"I hate him.

I freaking hate him.

He doesn't say anything nice to anyone.

Anything!

Not once.

I have been here for ten years, and I never heard that man compliment anyone.

Bet he doesn't say anything nice to his wife on their anniversary.

I worked my ass off cleaning this place up.

And then he comes by and asks me if I did anything while I was here.

How about this?

Fuck you.

And your fucking corvette or whatever expensive car he drives.

Did I tell you about the time he spoke to me for an hour about his car?

I was working and doing my job, which he didn't notice, and he goes on and on about his problems with his Corvette.

I'm like, dude, you don't pay me enough that I can buy a car like that."

He regrouped as his co-worker stood to lean up against the pole, listening.

Half interested in the rant because he works there.

Half-disinterested in the rant, because he doesn't want to work there for much longer.

"I can't stand him.

I can't.

I hate him so much.

It's a passion that is so bad, that dude,

I don't even know what I could do.

See this."

He picked up a block of wood.

"Right over his head, and no more problems.

That man's life could end, and no one in this company would even care."

"Some may even celebrate it."

The co-worker quickly replied and the refocused on giving advice.

"Don't let it bother you.

He is the boss.

He has to complain about the place or else no one will think he does anything around here.

My thinking, when he says something like that to me, is simple.

I am here from 6-2.

I do what I can till 2, which is what they pay me for.

It's not like they aren't paying me."

"Yeah... I mean."

"And then once it hits 2, I leave.

This job is not worth the stress."

"I know it isn't.

But it frustrates me so much.

You know?"

Out There

Two people stood at the opened door out into the foggy night.

"What is out there, you think?"

"Well, from what I gather it is one of two things."

God or Satan."

"Please.

Now you are talking like a crazy person.

If you want to talk like that, wait till there is some certainty to this all.

I don't need more of a reason to be nervous.

That fog in the distance is enough.

How far do you think that goes out?

Do you think it covers this whole town?

I bet it does."

"Will you just listen to me for a moment?"

"What sense is there in listening to a nut?"

"See if it's God, it is an all-powerful being who will judge your soul when you die, and probably knows everything about you.

Or it's Satan, who is doing everything in his power to lure you to his evil ways.

Either case, we are in a tough spot, with both beings have more power than we do."

"Or it can be nothing, and we are fools this whole time."

"Uh, yeah.

Let's hope it's that one."

Okay Jesus

I never told anybody this, but I might as well tell someone before I die, and you are the closest one near me now.

Sometimes before I go to bed, I think, "I hope Jesus is okay."

I don't know why this theological question pops into my over-analytical brain, for I don't attend church.

The spiritual ritual is too much of acceptance rather than thought engaging for my taste.

As if God did not make me with a brain to question and think of this world.

But to go along wherever the priests say to believe in.

I often found myself as I sat in the pews as the priests gave their sermons asking if Jesus would even be in the very spot of the gathering.

Where the masses are held.

Where heads bow to him.

No one thought that God would be a humble carpenter, and how did that work out for us?

Nor do I pray all that much, like so many Christians with bad knees asking for forgiveness or a raise in their job.

I know little of the rosary beads and the Stations of the Cross or other standards that church-goers know by heart.

I never paid much attention in Sunday school.

Despite all the presentation of an atheist, who would happily laugh at the idea of religion, I still think of this man's state of existence.

This faith in me knocks on my door just as I think it has left.

It's not like a guy like me can do much about it anyway, right?

I'm just a poet, with words, transcribing my experience for my fellow humans to read.

If anything I should be asking Jesus for help with something.

Like how to make a lot of money, so I don't have ever to work again.

Or whatever a preacher on TV would instruct you to pray for.

Every so often I'll be in bed and hope that he is doing okay.

I don't ask for anything from him.

I don't elaborate on why and how the question is posed.

Only that he, my Lord, is doing okay in heaven.

He gives me hope that all of this, the chaos and colossal mess of life, where we are debilitated by depression and ongoing conflict, and that salvation is never to be gained, will be okay.

Let me die unknown and never read by any reader.

Let these books be burned by ignorant masses who devalue the written word.

And let my works be erased like an error on a test written in pencil.

Who am I really?

I am nobody in terms of everything going on.

But Jesus.

He…

He can save us.

As long as he is okay, goodness has a chance to rule this world.

The Devil can't call this place home as long as he rises.

Jesus proves that love still wins.

And that it has a chance in this world.

And maybe that is all I want for myself, and everybody that I know,

A chance.

The Writing Salesman

Can I be honest with you?

Or as honest as a stranger can be to one another in written form?

I don't like other authors.

I know, I know.

I shouldn't say that.

Each line that I add to this piece is another writer acquaintance lost.

I might as well curse off other writers while I am at it.

I was thinking of titling my next piece F*** Writers

That may do it.

I am supposed to love all the other authors out there.

Give me a big hug, pat them on the back and talk of themes and stories.

"Your last novel truly inspired me to write a work in that genre that I changed how I am writing my current novel!"

Then we dip our quilted pens in some ink and discuss possible arcs and plot twists.

"I say, good sir, that character in scene 3 is vastly underdeveloped and too similar to the one in Act 2 Scene 4. Perhaps you should give the character a flashback so the audience can understand."

"Spot on point. I was thinking about making the two character's into one since they share so much."

I don't know why but that was never my style.

Perhaps I don't dislike authors, but the fakeness they give off when selling a book.

"My book is a bestseller." One writer will say to anyone listening.

"Oh, in what genre?" A curious listener may ask.

"Contemporary classic medical, psychological mystery thrillers with a woman lead between the ages of 20-35 and with 37 chapters and no prologue."

"Oh. Wow. Bestsellers are more specific than I realized."

I love when writers stick to the story.

It is the salesman in them that gets me.

Be a writer, not a salesman

What Every Poem Is About

Don't believe the hype from desperate writers, trying all they can to get you to buy their book.

Or all those reviewers with their verbose explanations for every poem in a collection.

Some with more words than the actual poems.

These people will give you sophisticated well thought out essays on what the poem is about.

How each verse, each phrase, each line, each word, means something that is worth reading.

They will attach some special words to the summary to get your interest as if you have never seen such a book before.

Such a plot, such a story, such a poem has never been attempted.

They will make up new meanings to explain the supposed great poems and stories for you to believe that the book is worth your time.

Don't believe any of it.

All poems are about the same thing.

I don't care if you are writing a love sonnet, a feminist poem with a picture, or a rhyming poem that Poe would be proud of.

All the poems are about us.

People are trying to figure what all of this is about.

Everything else you read is just another way of saying it.

Time Of Love

Can I love you more than time?

For what is time, but a man made idea?

A thought, a dream.

Time does not exist without man diligently recording it.

Or does it?

How do we, or any animal, or God, keep track of life, without the help of time?

I can't do it.

Every day I wake up and wonder what day of the week it is.

(It's Saturday)

Sometimes I'm asked what the date is.

(I normally don't know)

Time is feeble.

Time is a fraud.

A two-faced stranger seeking two identities.

Does my love reach higher than this?

What type of question is that?

Does golf have eighteen holes?

Are there nine innings in a baseball game?

Why question what is certain?

For whether it be today, tomorrow, the past, or the future, my love will be there.

I will still love you.

Time, the fickle friend of man, can leave.

It can stay.

It can be bent and broken so we no longer even know it as time.

You can break a man's watch, but you cannot break a man's heart.

The date does not matter for the date does not change how much I love you.

Time helps all record.

But it cannot put a measure for my love for you.

Pretending To Care

If I pretend to care, will you leave me alone?

If I act like I'm interested in whatever you say, will you leave me be?

See here is my problem, you're talking, and I don't remotely care of a single word you are saying.

They mean nothing to me.

I can't think of anything less interesting than what you are saying to me right now.

I'm sorry.

I don't want to be rude to you, but if I'm honest with myself, I wish you would go away.

I don't care about your opinion.

I never asked for it.

You are wasting your breath by speaking words to no one that is listening.

So here is the deal,

I'll stand here and pretend like your words mean something to me.

I'll respond with joy and fascination with the subject you present.

And when you are done talking I'll say goodbye and never see you again.

Does that sound fair?

No Depression

I have no depression to speak of.

No hurt in my mind.

No loss in my soul.

For I live a life without it.

How can I be depressed as I walk with Jesus?

As I bear the cross of the Lord?

As I pray to God?

Give me no pills, no dosage to cure me.

For what I have is greater than any prescription a doctor can write.

I have God.

He is the only medicine I'll ever need.

When I'm down, he lifts me.

When I'm hurt, he heals me.

When I'm lost, he finds me.

You won't find any sadness here, for God is here.

The Only Thing I Ever Liked About School

School at the end of the school year is not about lessons from the past, or learning new equations.

But leaving.

The last day of school is always tough.

As the sun beams down on you and your classmates.

And the AC is broken.

The teachers don't want to be there.

The students don't want to be there.

No one wants to be there.

Waiting...

Waiting...

Waiting...

And then it happens.

The bell rings.

You pick up your book bag and leave.

Not to go back.

No more tests.

No more classes.

No more assignments.

No more school.

Summer has begun.

You are free to do as you wish.

As the sun that melted your face off a little earlier welcomes you outside.

Almost as if it is saying, "Now it is time for some fun."

My Neighbor Is Mowing
The Lawn Right Now

I was going to write a great poem for you to read here

some

thing

like ee

cummings would write

where words

               would be

                              moved

          for meaning

But my neighbor is mowing the lawn right now

And it is pretty distracting

And I don't want to ask him to stop so that I could
write some poetry

So I guess I'm done with this poem

I'm not

                        waiting for

                                                him to

            stop mowing

Why My Books Will Never Be In Target (Or Any Other Mass Chain Store)

Why the hell do I care if my books get into Target?

I've been to that store many times.

I will even go a little later today to buy some groceries I need.

But who goes to Target for the books?

I don't.

And I'm a reader.

All the books in Target are for people who are buying cookies, tampons and rotisserie chicken and on their way to the checkout they see a book that catches their attention.

Perhaps the yellow background lures them over to the new young adult novel.

Or maybe it is the twenty percent red tag on the red bottom side of the book that does it.

So the person buys the book.

Not because they planned on reading it.

Or even want to, because they have plans for later today that do not include the book.

But because there is still some room in the cart.

Right by the two packs of water bottles and cereal boxes.

Plus the book is on sale, and with a membership deal, which the person has, the book will be really cheap.

Once I made a promise to myself to always buy a book at Target whenever I went to buy something I really needed, like toilet paper, or shaving cream.

I figured that I am an author and I should be trying to help my fellow authors as much as I can.

And putting down a few dollars for a book or two, may not be much, but is some contribution towards my peers.

It only took about four trips to Target for me to see that their book selections were limited and I would quickly run out of quality books to buy.

Also, let's be honest for a second.

The books in Target suck.

They are not classics.

They are not game changers.

They are not must-reads.

They are the contemporary books the store puts on their shelves so they can say that they sell books.

Not many of the books there are really worth reading.

Which makes my book the perfect candidate for the store.

After writing this, I realized I have all but killed any hope I ever had of getting my books in any of these stores.

Sweet New (Old) Style

A senior man well past his prime years and a young man ready for the world sat at park bench enjoying the summertime weather.

A beautiful woman walks by the two captivating the young man's eyes as he did not know where to look on her body.

The old man looks briefly but did not lose his eyes like the young man.

"Those Italian poets were too soon with their way of thinking."

Said the senior as he leaned backed into the chair.

"Uh-huh."

"I said those Italian poets were too soon with their way of thinking.

Saying that a woman's beauty is a gift from God.

That they are angels walking among man.

It was called "dolce stile Nuovo"

Which means a sweet new style and is a phrase from Dante's Purgatorio.

The poems by those Italians poets were written to glorify women.

Because the thought was that women were angels for man's salvation.

To love a woman is to love God then.

If those poets saw what women wore today.

They would claim that God is better than ever, and is spreading his love for all of us men to see.

We are to praise him for allowing us to see their beauty, which is his beauty."

He saw that his son was still staring off into the distance in which the woman walked.

"Man will always be enamored by the body of a woman.

No matter how far we come, a pretty girl can still melt a man's heart."

"Ah… yeah… sure."

"You didn't hear a word I said, did you?"

"Nope.

You think she'll come back around?"

Even They Leave

You know things are getting bad here on Earth when the angels and demons want nothing to do with us.

The angels, in all their glowing winged beauty, don't want to help us.

The demons, in their evil satanic terror, don't want to deceive us.

Both look at us, and shake their heads and say, "Yeah, that is not happening."

At a bus stop a demon, who turned away from manipulating humanity, sits next to an angel.

"So are you going to see the humans now?"

"No. Are you crazy?"

"Yeah. I tried that."

"Not worth it."

"Agreed."

The bus starts to go forward as they sit in silence.

"I hope this is the express line."

BUS STOP

Poet In A Park

Poets fit being in a park.

Daydreaming about all those illusive words.

Reflecting on life's biggest mysteries.

Making us all see things a little bit different.

Poets don't just walk through the park.

They notice the birds and can name them off the top of their head.

(since when did bird sightseers write verse?)

They notice the sounds.

I'm sorry, not the sounds, but the beauty of nature.

They notice the plants (because every poet is a botanist apparently)

And a million other ideas that no one thinks about when they go into a park.

No poet has ever walked in a park and thought the whole place looked like crap.

There is garbage all over.

The infield of the baseball field is full of grass.

And a part of the fence by the entrance is broken.

Poets don't go to those types of parks.

Not only do they go to recyclable, cleaned, fixed facilities, but they are profound when doing it.

I don't know why but the idea that a poet is in deep thought as they walk the tree-filled park is very common.

Yet how many poems are written in a park?

Or even by a tree?

As compared to, how many are written in a writer's office?

Because the image of a person peacefully walking a park path is more satisfying than the image of a person frantically filing papers and typing lines in the office.

You probably imagined that I wrote this in a park as you read this.

I didn't.

Joe's Dog

"Did you hear about Joe?"

"No. What of him?"

"His mom passed."

"Oh."

"And his sister and his dog. All in the same month."

"Damn…………………………………………………………………………… He really loved that dog."

"Yeah, he liked it more…"

"More than people. Who were the other two again?"

"His sister and mom."

"Yeah, that's sad too."

"Damn. He really loved that dog."

"Yeah. He did."

The Shortcut

I flipped through a writing magazine bored of the slow afternoon and of my repetitive writing.

Maybe some article can get the old' mind going.

Some quotes by Lewis or a story about O. Henry's life before becoming a writer.

But I find nothing.

On the page is an exercise about replacing the words in a story.

just		little			in order to
	like		that		
still		a bit/a lot		in addition to	
	then		very		
really		seem		of	
	but		because		see
saw		hear		hear	
	feel		felt		start

Any colloquial word or phrase you know you tend to overuse

I closed the magazine, still uninterested in writing a poem.

It looks like I am going to have to retire since I use the word just one too many times.

Day Teaching

"How's everything?"

"Not bad.

I'm getting the job at the school we used to go to."

"You mean the one where the teachers hated me?"

"Yeah.

And the last week of school where I was teaching was easy.

The teachers had to stay until three, even though the students were gone.

Me and three other teachers, who are girls our age, watched *Harry Potter*.

Because everyone needs to see that."

"If you like to see a British guy with a stick defeat an albino.

It takes too long.

At one point, I was hoping that Harry would save the day already.

So much for a protégé."

"We ordered pizza directly to the room."

"Are any of them cute?"

"Victoria is."

We also went to Six Flags.

Then the next week, we went to Splish Splash.

I got paid to spend a day with three women at Splish Splash."

"That's awesome."

I wonder how cute Victoria really is.

I bet she has a great smile.

Why am I writing poetry again instead of doing a job that has benefits like that?

I forget.

Real Reality

Do you ever stop and think to yourself, as you go through the daily motions, that all of this is not real?

You sitting down reading these words is nothing more than an elaborate dream.

A collective dream of many dreamers.

This is not a conspiracy.

It is true.

This world, this life, this experience, is not it, to the universe.

The world we live in, is at best, a passage to another world.

We may, or may not be allowed in, after our time here.

I don't care what religion you believe in,

A Christian with your Trinity.

A Buddhist and your path.

A Muslim and your law.

A Sikh and your "k's."

Or whatever else you follow.

You have to feel a bit strange when you stop and think about the whole idea.

You may not even be where you think you are right now.

You can't prove it, as you read this.

But we both know it is true.

There is nothing real about reality.

I'll Let You Decide What She Was Trying To Buy

An older fit woman walked into a store and saw a young man putting labels on the products.

She stared at the products until she finally addressed the worker.

"You work here right?"

"What do you need?"

"I need something long and hard. What I have won't work."

"Oh. How's this?"

He showed the woman a product he felt fit her vague description.

"This is okay.

Do you have anything thicker?"

"Ah…"

"See this is good but if I could use one a bit thicker and even longer, if you have it."

"It's hard enough? We have some soft kinds over there."

"Yeah.

Nice and hard.

This is good.

I have tried the soft before and I didn't like it.

Soft never lasts.

Hard is good.

A little more length would help me.

Some on the front and sides."

"The best I can say is that we have something like that but it is either much thicker or longer than what I showed you.

Not both."

"Let me see."

"Here."

He showed her the two products he was talking about.

"Oh yeah. I need something much bigger than that."

"In that case the best I can tell you is that you may find something larger in another part of the store."

He hesitated.

"For the product that is."

"Thanks."

I'll let the reader figure out what she was buying.

Walking By A School

I walk by a school getting my daily walk in.

Nesconsett.

Nes-con-sett?

Ne-scon-sett?

Nesc-ons-ett?

I don't know how to pronounce it.

I'm not from around here.

I walk past the small empty parking lot.

The place must be off for the summer.

The school looks private to me.

It isn't Catholic since I see no statues of saints.

It isn't Jewish since I see no stars.

(Although I am holding out on that one, since I do see
a lot of blue on the windows)

I bet this is a private school for all religions.

One of those new types of school that pretends all those old books say the same thing.

Which if anyone ever read them, can tell you, they don't.

(That is why they are different books)

The place has a rock by the cement path for its 95th anniversary.

Although they probably should make it 100 by now.

This is either a private Catholic school,

A private Jewish school,

Or a private other religion school.

I can't imagine this school being public.

I get to my car done with my walk.

1.5 miles, not bad.

The public school closed five years ago.

What I Think About Sometimes

"You know what I think about sometimes?

How was *Good Vibrations* left off of *Pet Sounds*?

Can you believe that?"

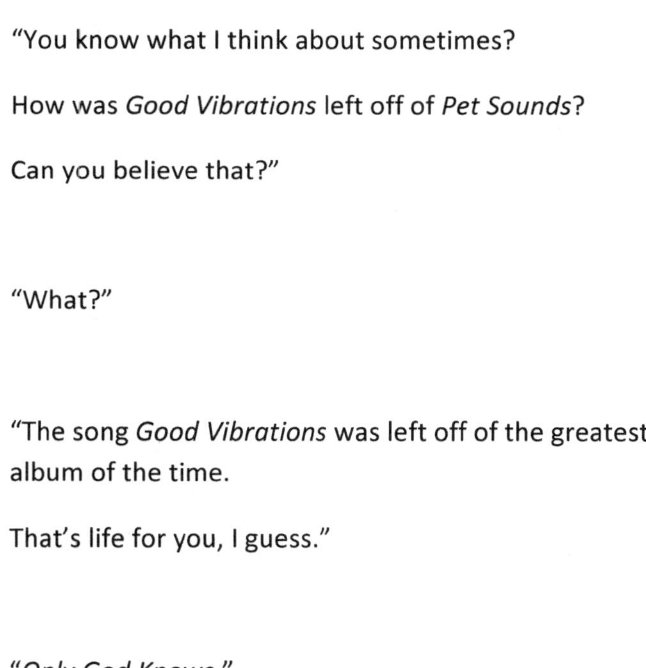

"What?"

"The song *Good Vibrations* was left off of the greatest album of the time.

That's life for you, I guess."

"*Only God Knows.*"

"I see what you did there.

I've been bed stricken for the past week.

I'll probably never walk again.

Yet all I can think about is something strange like that.

That album made the Beatles produce Srgt Pepper.

And we all know how that went.

Do you remember the picture frame we had in the old house of that cover?

Do you think if they released *Good Vibrations* on the album, that would have changed things?

Because although it is considered a classic today, it was not as well-received as their previous work."

"I don't know.

I just hope you are feeling better."

"I don't know what I'm supposed to feel.

Should I be sad, or angry, or something else?

I know I live in a world where the greatest album of all time didn't include the band's most popular song.

And the album that would take the title, later on, didn't release any singles.

And we think we have this all figured out.

The whole thing puts a smile on my face."

"That's good."

"I've heard a good amount of jokes in my day,

And I still say that God has the best sense of humor."

There Are Drag Racers In My Town, And I Don't Like It

Can the drag racers in my neighborhood get into a major crash already and die?

Nobody wants you around here.

Not me.

Not my neighbors on the block.

Not neighbors on any block in this town.

You, late at night with your engines and races driving for money (or whatever it is your race for) in overpriced cars that cost more than you.

I could sell the pieces of your car and then sell you and all your pieces and get more for your car.

You guys are probably the same jackasses who don't allow me on the highway right away.

Who almost cause accidents by simply how you drive.

Either leave.

(There are other roads in other towns that you can race on.

My town is not the only town that exists!

I'm sure they will welcome your noise as much as we do.)

Or die.

(A pileup of a few cars that accidentally collide when racing, or separate crashes will do.)

I don't care which.

Whatever gets you to stop.

I'm only writing this because I know I'm not the only one in the town who hates you.

No one hears your races and thinks

"Yes! We have drag racers here! I drove by those guys on the highway, and they're the best!"

We all think that whoever is driving those cars will get into an accident one day.

Some, like me, would even prefer it.

Family Connection

A family member of mine works for a major book publishing company.

Naturally, when my other family members saw her, they informed her of me and my books.

"He writes."

"Oh?"

"Yeah. Can you help him?"

"No."

"Why not?"

"He needs an agent if he wants to be seen by the big publishers."

"Oh."

So much for that great family connection.

You Decide

Are poems visual?

spoken Or

IF

I

make

this

visual

Does

it   **matter?**

Or are elaborate rhymes and quotable prose what captivates you?

IS THIS MEANT TO

BE SEEN

Or only spoken?

I'll let you decide.

Weird Sport

So the match takes place on Friday in England,

where the courts are grass,

is being reffed by a man from France,

where the courts are clay,

as a right-handed Serbian,

ranked number twelve,

who got injured in Australia,

where the courts are hard,

plays a left-handed Spaniard,

ranked number two,

who is trying to take the number one spot from a Swede,

who excels on all courts.

The winner plays on Sunday,

a right-handed South African,

ranked number eight,

who beat a right-handed American,

ranked number nine.

This is a really weird sport.

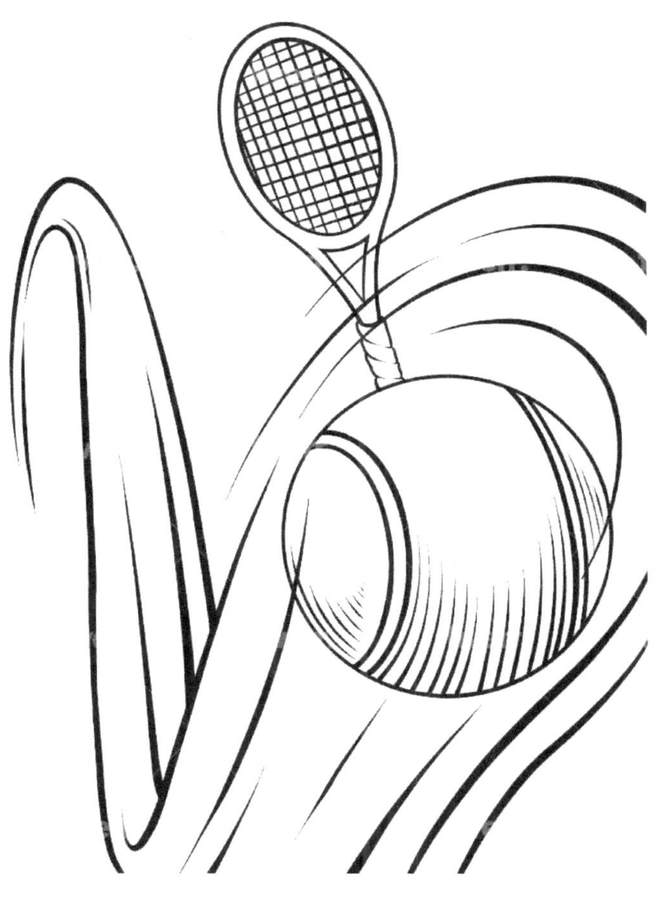

The Only Murder I Ever Committed

I must confess to a murder that I committed a few years back.

On an easy-going Saturday afternoon, I took a kid outside in the backyard and shot him in the head.

He was getting in my way with all his childish behaviors and silly thoughts.

What else was I supposed to do?

Society demands that I be an adult.

Grown-ups run the world, not kids.

And since I realized that I couldn't be a kid forever, I took it upon myself to end my childhood.

"I'm sorry."

I said to the innocence in me as we stood in the back.

"I have to do this.

I will not survive in this world if I allow you to keep living."

The kid stared at me with his toy truck in hand.

"I like sand. Sand is fun."

"Don't! Don't look at me!" I demanded.

"Ah. Okay. I'll go play in the sandbox."

"No! You have to stay here!"

"But why?"

Two shots went off.

"I won't make it if all I think about is fun and sand.

I have to grow up."

Tears ran down my face for the victim.

"I'm so sorry. I had to do this."

I went back inside and let the corpse of the child dry out in the sun.

We had no memorial service for the child.

No funeral.

No eulogy.

Nothing.

If you go back there today, you wouldn't even know a crime took place.

Being Seen

Poems are meant to be

V-I-S-U-A-L

o

Œ

t

Œ

r

ℜ

e

a

Viewednotread

D

i　　　　　*i*

i

i

~~NOT~~

~~EVEN   QUOTED~~

At least that is what I was told.

Idiots

I have a word for writers who are intimidated by the blank page in front of them.

Who can't gather the proper phrases to craft their story?

Who are stuck with the book they are writing.

Idiot.

(I admit that this word can be followed by demeaning questions for the individual.)

They are the same people who make a simple job assignment so much more difficult than it has to be.

Then expect a raise when they do it.

Writing is simple.

You get an idea.

You put down the idea.

Then you put down words to explain the idea.

Just like how the report your boss gave you to revise is easy.

Don't pretend like it isn't.

Stupid people tend to make things harder than they have to be.

If you find it difficult then, I have a word for you.

Idiot.

Beat Of A Howl

I only know one of two things about Allen Ginsberg.

1. The girl I grew up with in school was crazy about him.

She was a hipster.

2. He was Jewish.

The name gives it away.

I stare at the cover of the book of the poet I heard only in passing.

The guy has his hairy stomach hanging out from his unbuttoned shirt.

That's kind of weird.

I don't trust a man who is shirtless on his own book cover.

He looks like that actor from the movie I saw once.

It wasn't a great movie, and he didn't even have a big role in it.

But he looks just like that guy.

What was that guy's name again?

Ah, whatever.

It says he was a part of the Beat Generation.

Which I'm sure means something to someone.

Beat?

Like the food?

So there is a whole generation of writers known for their diet?

Or is that beet?

So they were winners (or good at beating people)?

Is that it?

I guess that is cool.

Writers have to define their generations cause if they don't, no one will.

Fitzgerald was lost.

Ginsberg was beat.

So what am I then?

I'm a part of the generation that is so aware of the labels given to the former generations that we don't even give ourselves a name.

This means we are so sophisticated we don't get bogged down by the petty names or titles that society bestows upon us.

Or we have no idea what to call ourselves.

Maybe it is to rebel against the corrupt system we feel only holds us down culturally, and financially.

Or you know... something.

The book says he wrote a poetic masterpiece, *Howl*.

Howl?

Why don't I know this poem?

(I probably should)

I turn to the page of the poem.

It is multiple pages long and has way too many words for me to give it much thought.

I closed the book.

I'll leave Ginsberg to that hipster girl I knew in school.

I Don't See Why Death Needs To Be Scary

I don't get Death.

Why does he have to scare me?

I'm already dead, at that point.

He won.

I'm leaving the world.

And he feels the urge to scare the crap out of me with a scythe and bones.

Really, Death?

Is that needed?

If there was such a thing as an asshole move for the other world entities, Death being scary is one of them

Scary, or not, people are still gonna die.

It's not like Death has to worry about that.

What sort of weird mental problem does Death have that makes him do this?

Does Death have daddy issues he'd like to talk about?

Maybe he feels overwhelmed by all the dead people and needs a vacation.

Or maybe he hates his job and is doing everything he can to be fired, but it just hasn't happened yet.

So when Death decided he would deal with people, he thought the best appearance would be terrifying.

That's the look he chose?

His job is to deal with people or at least dead ones,

And he chose to look the one way, that makes no one want to deal with him.

When I die, I'm not going to be afraid of Death.

Rather I'll roll my eyes at his inappropriate attire and say,

"Let's get this over with."

And if he gives me attitude, I'm going to go back at him.

"Really Death?

I'm not the one who is carrying around a scythe dealing with dead people.

I only have to do this once.

You have to do this all the time.

You can't try to scare me.

I knew I was going to die all along."

I wonder if Death reads poetry.

Politics

Did you hear about the new policy?

What new policy?

You know the one they just passed.

Oh yeah. That one.

What do you think?

It's stupid.

How am I
going to eat, or work?

It will ruin
everything. Politicians
are clueless.

Do you normally follow politics?

No.

Me neither.

The Meeting That Would Have Changed Everything

-

会议本来会改变一切

A Chinese explorer approached a merchant with the hopes of seeing this place known as Rome in person.

The merchant, who had never been to Rome, was moving around the last of his items and ready to leave the market for the day.

"Excuse me, do you know where Rome is?"

"Rome the capital, or the city?"

"What's the difference?"

"They are different places."

He picked up the last bit of rope from the table and tried his best to get by the questioner.

"Excuse me."

The Chinese explorer was speechless.

Two Romes?

The emperor only told him of one Rome.

Is this empire so great that it has two cities for its title?

Is that why it's so heralded in the west?

Two Romes?

Nobody mentioned anything about two Romes.

I was only told to find one.

"I…. I… I was only asked to arrive in Rome. I'm trying to find Rome."

"We all are buddy."

He tightened up the rope on his camel.

"Cui bono."

"Fine. Where is the capital then?"

He got on his camel.

"That'll take you up to two years to get to if you go by boat.

Carpe diem."

He muttered to his tired self.

"Oh."

"Send my regards to Caesar.

The bastard still owes me money from last year's taxes.

He is on all the coins yet still can't pay me back.

The great city of Rome, man I'll tell ya."

The Chinese explorer dejected by the news left the market and headed back to his homeland.

The city of Rome was only a mere forty day trip by land.

A Therapist's Words

"I don't know doc.

What's wrong with me?

I feel okay.

I feel fine.

But I ...

"How is that writing career coming along?"

"Good. Good.

I am starting a publishing company.

Things are looking up there.

But I still...

I don't know.

I still feel lost."

"Really?"

"Yeah."

"Your dilemma is that you have used writing to find purpose in yourself and this world,

For even you said that you don't write for the money or the fame,

When you were a young man, this approach worked to give you a contemporary identity,

But as you grow, you are losing sight of yourself.

Let me ask you;

Are you, only your words, the verse you put on a piece of paper?

Or is there more to you than a book?"

"Is there?"

"You tell me."

"I'm afraid if I stop writing, I will have to confront who I really am."

"And who is that?"

"A lonely lost man, who seeks literature as his escape from his problems."

"So why don't you stop?"

"I can't."

"Why not?"

"It's all I know.

Without words to rule my life, I have no life."

"So you write?"

"Yeah."

"You question,

You seek.

You explore.

You create.

You imagine.

Informing, educating, and amusing readers.

All the while missing the one true person who needs your writing the most,

You."

"The very tool I use to show off my observations and opinions of the world, I can't use on myself."

"Words are not the problem here."

"I am."

"You think you can write your way out of it.

Like you have for every other topic or idea you have ever have.

Don't have a poem to write?

Mock the art of poetry by writing about how you can't write a poem!

Don't like the college you are in?

Write a novel about your experiences!

Learn something new about Ancient Rome?

Make that the title of your next book!

But you....

You are not a character.

You are not writing a story.

You are trying to find who you are."

"And that can't happen unless I give up writing."

"As long as you write, you will drown your own confusion into stories, rather than confronting them head-on."

"What would you say, if I told you, I already, kind of, by accident, wrote of this exchange? "

"You didn't."

"No?"

"Oh, Jesus Christ."

Blaming Myself

I blame you.

I blame them.

I blame it.

I blame him.

I blame her.

I blame you.

I blame God.

I blame Allah.

I blame Buddha.

I blame Jesus.

I blame Moses.

I blame Shakespeare.

I blame Tao.

I blame Confucius.

I blame Plato.

I blame you.

I blame my family.

I blame my father.

I blame my mother.

I blame my brother.

I blame my sister.

I blame my other brother.

I blame my step-father.

I blame my step-mother.

I blame you (again)

I blame the church.

I blame the temple.

I blame the mosque.

I blame the synagogue.

I blame the priest.

I blame the minister.

I blame the pope.

I blame the deacon.

I blame the monk.

I blame the rabbi.

I blame you (again)

I blame the schools.

I blame the colleges.

I blame my teacher.

I blame my English teacher.

I blame my science teacher.

I blame my math teacher.

I blame my gym teacher.

I blame my history teacher.

I blame some of my teachers.

I blame all of my teachers.

I blame you (again)

I blame life.

I blame death.

I blame love.

I blame hate.

I blame destiny.

I blame the money.

I blame poverty.

I blame greed.

I blame wealth.

I blame ignorance.

I blame knowledge.

I blame power.

I blame you (again)

I blame my weight.

I blame my height.

I blame my hair.

I blame my face.

I blame my nationality.

I blame my race.

I blame my color.

I blame my IQ.

I blame you (again)

I blame the politicians.

I blame the senator.

I blame the governor.

I blame the president.

I blame the lawyers.

I blame the judges.

I blame the voters.

I blame the Constitution.

I blame Lincoln.

I blame Jefferson.

I blame you (again)

I blame the system.

I blame the news.

I blame the newspapers.

I blame the books.

I blame the culture.

I blame the internet.

I blame social media.

I blame you (again)

All of this is to blame for where I am.

Do I blame myself?

What kind of stupid question is that?

Done With Another Good Poem

Type. Type. Type

Words. Words. Words.

Sentence. Sentence. Sentence.

Line. Line. Line.

Done.

Another good poem written.

Loving You

I'm sorry I can't be the man you want me to be.

But...

I will never give you the love you deserve.

My true love is my career.

And I will never devote my time to you as I should.

It's not fair for me to keep you then.

All to myself.

Pretending I will love you.

I won't.

I love all about you.

But as far as actually loving you.

I'm sorry, I can't do that.

My Other Stuff

Somewhere along the line, if I'm lucky, I'll be known for a book by the masses.

And this...

Yes...

This...

Will be known as the other stuff I wrote.

That only the real fans know of.

Stuff that was okay.

Good, but not me (or the idea of me)

If you are a real fan of mine, you'll know this and appreciate how this helped me develop into the idea that society has of me.

And you even argue how my other stuff is better than my more famous work.

It was more real.

More me.

Not for the masses anyway.

Look at you, being a devoted fan and all.

I like it.

Because I'm not writing this I guess.

I only write like that book that I wrote that one time.

All that other stuff I wrote, isn't what people think of when they think of me, so that doesn't count.

So it's that....

Or this poem is wishful thinking by an out of his head writer.

In that case, all my stuff is my other stuff, and I have nothing to worry about.

Not Even A Stool

As I walked by the Apple Store in the mall, I couldn't help but mock it.

That place has no chairs inside.

Not one.

How can people not see that they are only trying to sell something?

That that will point out the good features in the product for sale to go through, as they "accidentally" forgot the other parts that will burden the buyer.

Are people really that stupid?

I paused.

Yeah.

Yeah. They are.

I then walked by another store selling products that a person does not need.

Items meant to cover up the isolation you feel in your own life.

The confusion you have in your place in the world.

Here take a jacket.

That will do the trick.

Better yet, take five.

No amount of purchases can help you accept your place in this life.

No great deals.

No coupons.

No discounts.

Nothing.

Everyone goes to the mall for something yet no one finds what they are truly looking for.

Wait a minute.

There are no chairs anywhere in this mall.

Except for the food court and vendors. (and those don't count)

The mall is designed for people to become mindless consumers.

Always standing, always buying.

Never thinking, never reflecting.

And you know what?

It's working.

Once you find comfort in your identity, no matter how wrong it is, you will find it difficult to let that part of you go.

This is who we are.

This is what we do.

We have to view ourselves in the mirror at some point and stop lying about ourselves.

We can talk about morality and ideas, and philosophy all we want.

But look around you…

Does it really look like anybody cares about those things?

Should I Use My Poetry to Bang Chicks?

As I listen to my co-worker describe his multiple side chicks

(I'll leave his actual details to your imagination)

I couldn't help, but think I'm doing this all wrong.

I'm a poet.

I'm the one who can quote Shakespeare.

Who reads Poe and Austen.

Who knows of love poems.

Hell, I've written some.

I'm the one writing the words the women readers like.

So....

Why am I not using my poetry to bang every girl I can?

....

Because...

That would be....

Wrong.

That wouldn't be right.

To make up fake love ballads just to get some.

To create wordy poems for a girl to fall for me.

To use my writing as a tool of seduction.

No...

I won't resort to that.

My co-worker is a jackass.

He is cheating on his girlfriend and is carelessly breaking girl's hearts.

To him, a naked woman is worth a broken heart.

I always thought I was a better man than that.

I'm still trying to be.

Tomorrow I'll Be 90

Tomorrow I'll be 90.

I am done with my life.

You are done with these words.

You are done with living.

And content with myself.

And my place.

Life has thrown all it can look at me.

Yet here I sit.

Quiet, relaxing in a chair.

Prepared for Death.

For my good fight is over.

Life has thrown all it can look at me.

And I still made it.

I'll laugh at my own life.

Smile at the good times.

Cry over the sad times.

But I'll be content, with it all.

Tomorrow I'll be 90.

No more wiser.

No more smarter.

Than I am now.

But I am satisfied with my life.

I lived the life I wished to live.

Of all the battles I fought, only time has been the victor.

And for that, I am eternally grateful.

Tomorrow I'll be 90.

And I'm okay with that.

Those Who Know

Those who know the true words to this poem know
that they are not written here.

Not in English.

不是中文

ليس باللغة العربية

pas en français

non in italiano

no en español

日本人ではない

ne u hrvatskom

בעברית לא

Non latine

όχι στα ελληνικά

не по-русски

pa nan Kreyòl ayisyen

한국인이 아니야.

não em portugues

Not in any language.

The real words in this poem don't have to be written.

If you try to read them, you never will.

Why I Am In Hell

Now if I was Satan,

What would I do?

I'd create a false world,

Where I am beloved.

All pray to me.

And there is no escape from my world.

Everyone would be stuck there.

No one would ever meet God in this world I created.

Whose title I would gladly take on.

I live in a false world,

Where God is beloved.

All pray to him.

There is no escape from this world.

No one has ever met God, or even proved he exists.

Son of a bitch.

Am I in hell?

Think about it.

If I were in hell, the Devil would never want me to think I was there.

He'd create a lie so rich that I'd mistake it for truth.

Please Don't Read Me

Words have a life of their own.

They travel, like a disease that flows through your veins.

But a handshake will not spread it.

Nor will a rat on a boat.

But this page will.

The words latch onto your feeble mind.

And they don't leave.

Until you forget them.

But you won't forget them

Because you like them.

And want more.

So the disease becomes the cure.

And who willfully put their down their own thoughts on this messy napkin, this unclean cloth?

I did.

And I regret it.

It takes a part of me to write this.

I give you a piece of myself with each confession, each construct, each concept.

So am not living as long as these words are read?

Now the prospect of immortality is quite welcoming.

But what happens when I die?

My soul, to which I bared before you, can't rest.

Because I wrote these words.

I left my sickness on the page that you gladly gave to everyone you know.

As you read my words, my soul speaks.

Please don't read this.

For my soul will never get rest as long as this verse lives.

Vacation

I need a nap.

Then a cup of coffee.

Then a protein bar.

Then another nap.

Then a five hour energy drink.

Then another cup of....

I need a vacation.

Statistics For An Atheist

Atheists are very big on numbers and statistics.

Whenever I hear one talk, I always ask for them to give me a calculator or a ruler.

Theirs works better than mine.

"Shows me the facts!"

They yell at me.

"Show me the money!"

I respond, hoping they have a few bucks on them, and a sense of humor.

They never do.

The only way for atheists to be in the majority would be having 51 percent of the world's population.

There are over 8 billion people in the world. (as of this writing)

So 4.1 billion have to not be apart of religion for atheists to have a reasonable chance.

Let's run the numbers.

There are over 2 billion Christians in the world.

1.5 billion Muslims.

750 Hindus.

They are the big players.

2 +1.5 + .75 = 4.25 billion

And that is not including other religions.

Yet atheists like to go around as if they are the majority.

But if over 51 percent of people claim to be a part of a religion.

That means that the only way for atheists to have the majority is if the people from those religions are lying.

But how can you prove that anyway?

Is there a sect to each religion for those who are there for show?

"Oh, I don't believe in any of this.

I am here for the free food and nice buildings.

Don't mind me."

Commitment to a religion doesn't change the fact that the person is still a part of the religion.

Bad Christian, good Christian, you're still a Christian.

Atheists will say that it is an establishment built on conformity and that you are not apart of the religion because you believe, but because you have to.

Which is kind of insulting, when you think about it?

I'd like to think people are in the religion because they actually believe in the religion.

I could be off on this.

So how are you going to explain that most people are attached to religions, while most of us are atheists too?

Unless you go off of speculation rather than actual concrete facts.

And you imagine that all those believers are like you, with their ideas, without any shred of proof on your part.

Anyone who is apart of religion is lying and is an atheist, just pretending to be religious.

Nah.

Atheists wouldn't do that.

Stupid Lost Idiot

Bad things make me happy.

I am proud to be a disappointment.

Failure in life is why I continue mine.

I am excited to be a loser.

To be rude to kindness.

I like letting myself and others down.

To trip progress down the stairs.

To be given advice and ignore it.

To mock peace and hope.

I've tried being good but didn't care for it.

Only when I'm down, do I feel up.

I enjoy being a stupid lost idiot.

I can't help it.

Better Late Than Never

Her name was Megan.

She is a nurse who is fine breaking ribs to save a life.

Death with good ribs is much worse than living with broken ones.

She is a possible narcoleptic because she has slept on two dates.

Although I don't know how much sitting on the couch watching a series on Netflix constitutes as a date.

I attribute this, (her sleeping, not her choice of dates) to her twelve-hour nurse shift lifestyle, but her nickname of Rip Van Wrinkle suggests that her fellow nurses think there is a deeper cause to her naps.

Rather than her disinterest in her dates.

And here I am.

I am going on and on about her.

Like I will see her tomorrow.

And we will....

Stop.

Stop right now.

I know how this game plays.

And I always lose.

I can't stop thinking about her for a while.

And she and I never see each other again.

My storytelling takes over, and I imagine a way that we cross paths and fall in love.

Some bullshit story that can't happen.

Then I think about going to see her where she works (at the hospital)

And I stop.

My self-doubt is never getting me out of the front door.

Then, as my mind comes back to my empty reality, my journey with her will slowly evaporate with my past thoughts of her.

Her face being slowly altered with time.

Our conversation is slightly vaguer.

Until she is no longer found in my own memory.

Until this poem is all that is left.

I'm over the idea of a girl that I like, reading my work, and being impressed by my words.

I lie to myself and pretend that they will.

"Women loved Poe."

An old writing teacher remarked one time.

I'm not Poe, and I never will be.

I have yet to meet a friend I met already, who reads me and then wants to see me again.

"Oh, I love that poem you wrote!

Do you want to go out sometime?"

They never say.

This is our second date, Megan.

We went out to a nice Italian restaurant.

I ordered a shrimp pasta with clam sauce, and you ordered some chicken parmesan.

During our conversation, you told me of how you were intimidated by one of the other nurses after one of the new interns was performing CPR improperly.

I then told you how that Michael Jackson song had the words, Annie, in it, because that is what the dummy was called back then.

You found that amusing.

And here I go again.

My mind loving you more than I ever will.

I don't want to end here.

Out of thoughts.

And out of love.

But what else am I to do?

I don't have you.

Which makes all the rest seem pointless.

Maybe it is best to forget I ever even met you.

I'm Only Writing This Because My Laptop Just Died

My laptop just died.

So I am dead right now.

Yeah, you are reading the words of a dead man.

A zombie, a corpse brought back from the dead.

Hurry, run, before I eat your brains!

I'm kidding.

If I were a zombie, I wouldn't eat your brains.

I would dance though.

My laptop stores info I use.

If it dies, I have no access to the information.

I don't know how to think without that info.

If my laptop is dead, so am I.

What do you think I would have said back when they built the pyramids or some other architectural design we will never accomplish in this modern age?

(Because of labor restrictions more than anything else)

I am only writing this because the stone tablet I originally wrote on ran out of the room.

I knew I should have been more careful!

Nevermind that.

No one back then in their right mind would have jotted down irreverent thoughts like this.

By the time they got to the second symbol, they'd give up.

Which is what I feel like doing now.

I really have to find an outlet.

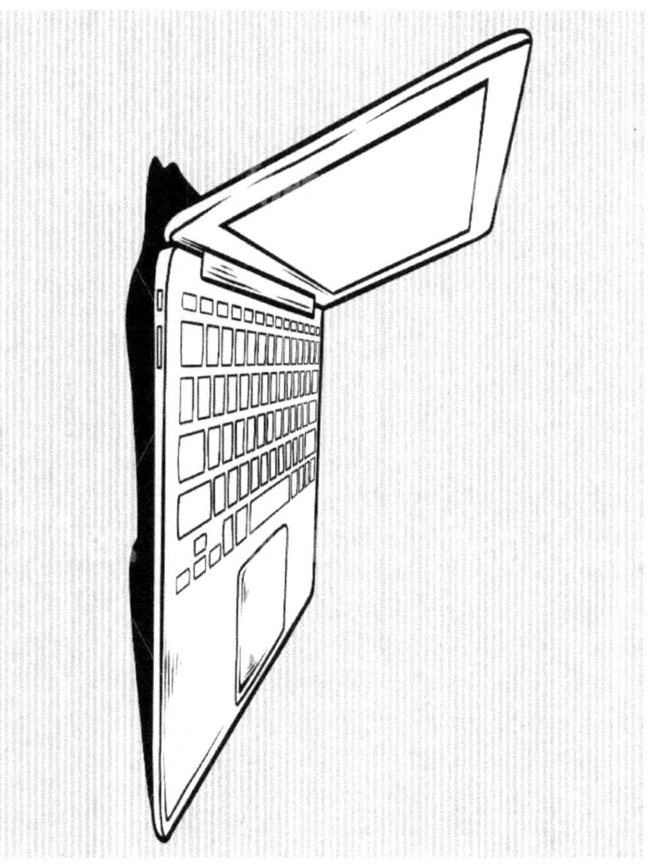

On The Mountain Top

You will find me on the mountain top.

As I wait.

For what?

Even I don't know.

Is it for the Holy Grail I still seek?

For that elusive treasure to meet me atop this lonely icicle?

Or have I found out the truth to my conquest and wish to see no more?

It was all a lie.

All I did, all I accomplished, all I am.

How did I ever believe it in the beginning?

Or am I here for an unknown purpose even to myself?

Has fate led me here like directions on a map?

And even I, don't know why I'm here.

I will not say.

Dots are my answer to you.

As they were to everyone.

I will only wait.

On the mountain top.

As the cold snow melts my feet, the chill cools my breath, and the mountain consumes me.

I will wait.

Day after day.

Month by month.

Year after year.

Until I get what I came up here for.

If you ever need to find me,

You know where I'll be.

What To Learn

What do I need to learn?

NOOOOOOOOOOOOOOOOO!

Don't ask me that.

I hate learning.

I always tend to forget most of it.

Whether I am learning a new sport, a new game, or a new skill.

Most of it goes away like I never even learned it at all.

And that is always the stuff I need to remember.

The stuff that people ask about.

Why am I never asked questions about the things that I do remember?

Don't ask me what I need to learn!

Because I don't know.

I either never knew it, or just forgot it.

I hate learning.

It's why I am so forgetful.

I Should Have Gone To Business School

I'm telling ya, I should have learned business, not writing.

Profits, not poems.

Margins, not manuscripts.

Stocks, not symbols.

I should have learned a way to make some money.

Maybe something with stocks, or becoming an accountant, or something where the job was to make money.

So I was set for life.

I am not writing.

Not this.

Screw writing.

There is no money in this.

Do you know how many books I have to sell to make what I could if I invested in smart stocks?

I'm not gonna think too much about it, or I'll go mad.

See, you will read this and think this is a joke.

That I am only trying to be funny.

To brighten up your day with my witty observation.

I'm not kidding.

I really should have gone to business school, and learned how to make some money.

I am not writing.

Being a writer was a mistake.

I Never Want To Become Myself

I sit in Barnes and Noble,

staring at my laptop,

learning the classics.

Or at least trying to.

Sophocles.

Shakespeare.

Eliot.

Twain.

Orwell.

Oh Jesus, this list is too long.

Does anybody know all of these people?

My mind wanders, and I realize that the radio is not playing its usual Broadway hits.

Music out of place for the senior crowd that is here.

One senior always points out the misplacement of the Broadway songs.

"Where are we? No one wants to hear that!"

Yet they are played every day.

The cute worker is over by the magazine's section restocking cooking or whatever magazine that needs to be replaced.

And that list is still on my screen.

Stop mocking me, Poe!

I still get upset that the bastard died at 40, and somehow wrote so much.

What did he live at his desk?

That dude had written more by the time he got to forty than most writers do in their lifestyle.

And...

And it was good.

Screw him.

Three men behind me start to speak of various topics that interest old men.

Sports, politics, and the like.

All speak with experts in the fields that they have no experience in.

Certainty is their tone.

They have no stake in the sports teams and have never run for office.

Yet, they know so much about it.

I try to focus on the list, but the old guy's ignorant comments get to me.

And when I'm not eavesdropping, I'm staring at the worker.

Screw you, Plato!

Like you never got distracted before.

He didn't die young, so I don't get unnecessarily mad at him.

I begin a rebuttal in my head to the old men's points.

One that makes perfect sense to me.

I hold my tongue.

One must never try to convince an ignorant stranger of his views.

Unless you want to waste your time.

A few minutes later.

And many odd remarks after.

The three old men get up.

Fittingly jazz is put on the radio.

Jazz, the genre of music, that never gets to the point.

I hear one of the old guys say to another.

"We once again got nothing done."

I say that to my buddy too (probably too much, now that I think of it)

But when I do, I know that I am going to get things done later on.

I don't actually plan on getting nothing done.

They leave.

And I am left with my list.

Camus.

Huxley.

Dumas.

Fitzgerald

Verne.

Damn, all these writers of the past who wrote so many words.

They were all so selfish!

I am only thinking about their works!

What about the reader who has to spend time reading them?

Ha! I bet you never thought of that Shakespeare!

(Actually, I think he did. Nevermind)

I shut my laptop and head towards my car.

Once again, wasting what was supposed to be a productive day of writing.

Maybe one day, I'll write words that make sense.

As I put my bag in my car, I recall of the conversation of the seniors.

Am I going to become one of those old guys one day?

I am talking about sports, politics and the like, in a certain tone.

As a young man sits next to me rolling his eyes.

Stupid old men. They don't get it.

I then joke to my buddies about how useless our conversation was.

Never once acknowledging the overworked youngster sitting next to me, who politely didn't interrupt our discussion.

My only hope is that maybe the young writer will be as frustrated with Poe as I was once.

That guy did write a lot of words.

COFFEE

Pop Doesn't Exist

Sometimes when I turn on the radio and hear a song, I imagine what the future will say of us, and the music I listen to.

(I can already tell you that I don't listen to that song!)

What music did they listen to?

Pop.

Pop?

Popular.

Oh. I thought that was the sound it made.

No. It was what most
people listened to them.

Oh....

They didn't overthink it.

So anything could be pop as long as it's popular?

Theoretically, yes.

So they had no idea what they were listening to?

Yeah, basically.

Pop as a genre does not exist.

Because it is based upon the number of the audience, not the style.

Bestseller is not a genre of literature.

Blockbuster is not a genre of film.

Why?

Because anything can be a bestseller or a blockbuster!

So why does pop get its own genre?

Who knows?

Maybe the people in the future will have the answer.

I Have A Hard Time Writing About Love When There Are People Around

I'm uncomfortable writing about love as I sit in a half-filled café,

Coffee brewing,

People talking,

Music playing.

Love; you know the one with the heart.

Rings and red.

Valentine's and chocolate.

All that stuff that writers, musicians and every other artist in between, love to write about.

I don't know why.

Either artist is secretly the best lovers and are sharing their untapped wisdom with all of us.

Or they are pathetic losers who are too damn horny
to write about anything else.

I plead the fifth here.

I don't know why I'm uncomfortable with writing this.

I wrote about murdering someone the other day.

Murder; you know the one with….

Hmmm.

This doesn't work for murder.

Anyway, you get the point.

It's not like I'm writing this as a stranger stares
intently at me.

I know that I am writing (or not writing) a love poem.

Damn perceptive bastard.

Love poems require you to take a knife out and bleed.

Hoping that blood will get you to say something you
actually mean.

Some writers take this literally, which just adds to the whole experience.

(A little too much)

Love poems require I go there.

You know the place.

Where the therapists would shake their heads at me, wondering what the hell I'm doing.

Where my friend's question if I have problems that I have been hiding.

And that my girl has to accept as strange faults in me if she is going to be with me.

I guess that is why they say forever and not just over 100 years.

That place.

We all have it.

I'm not the only who gets that way.

Where we ask questions that philosophers pretend to have the answer to.

Who am I?

What am I doing here?

Why am I even here?

Those fun questions.

And then that eventually gets me to love.

Not that word again.

Like I don't hear those artists talk about it enough!

Love;

We all want it.

We all need it.

Yet none of us understand it.

You gotta love, love.

I'm going to stop writing this because I'm not comfortable going forward.

That coffee brewer is pretty loud.

And that old lady across the room hasn't stopped staring at me!

I started this by saying that I didn't want to write it.

The café is a bad place to bleed your heart out.

And I still say it is.

Just A Man

This poem, this book, this work,

is only words by a man and his pen.

That's all they ever were and ever will be.

Not something to remember.

Not something to teach.

Not even something to read.

A man and his pen.

That's all this is.

Don't let anyone else tell you otherwise.

Micropoetry Sucks

That's right.

I said it.

It sucks.

Micropetry is the name of that "poem" you read on Instagram that took you five seconds.

Which is great.

We named it.

Goddamnit.

Don't name the animal you plan to kill.

Now we are going to justify and glorify its existence.

As if it is good.

As if we need it.

As if we want it.

But it's not.

It sucks.

I read an article where the "poet" said he had twenty poems in his head by the end of the interview.

Twenty.

Give me a break.

The bastard writes quotes that paraphrase Vince Lombardi or Marilyn Monroe,

And I'm supposed to be impressed.

"Don't ever underestimate the heart of a champion."

That wasn't me.

That was Rudy T.

And it is not a poem.

It's a line.

These fake poets have to stop with this micropoetry.

It sucks.

I thought poets were the rebels of society, the voices of a generation.

And...

We have micropoetry.

Goddamnit.

That micro poem you love so much (it's okay I won't tell anyone)

That has eight lines and only five words,

That is what the future will think we thought of ourselves and the world.

It sucks.

We didn't think.

Why?

Thinking is hard.

People don't like hard things.

So we all want to read the easy work.

Talk about how you cried in a line and then have a picture of a tear.

Mention how you are hurt with a ripped rose on the page.

Or bring up how alone you are with a black shadow next to the line.

Wait…

I think I have a quote for this.

I mean a poem.

"I think I thought I saw you tried."

Also not me.

That was said by R.E.M., the band, not the sleep cycle.

And is also a likely candidate for a micro poem.

But that is not a poem.

It's a line.

No one wants to say it.

No one wants to admit it.

Because there is nothing to gain from such a statement.

The writers know that a long poem won't be read,
and figure if this is what is read, then so be it.

Rather be read writing crap, then not read at all.

And the readers want a quick fix.

The easy read that they can understand in one glance
on their way to the game.

Or that they can skim while watching Netflix.

And so we have micropoetry.

The fast food version of poetry.

The pop of poetry.

It's simple, it's easy, and most importantly, it's
popular.

If we are going to be a society of non-thinkers than
we deserve not to be thought of at all.

Homeless Co-Worker

My co-worker is homeless.

And I don't know what to do about it.

I see the guy once a week.

We share a few laughs over stuff.

Get done early, grab a bite and then go our separate ways.

I only know he's homeless because another co-worker told me.

I don't know if I should bring it up or let it go.

An old buddy of mine is depressed.

And I don't know what to do about it.

I hung out with him in school every so often.

We'd share a few laughs over stuff.

Go to class, have lunch together and then go our separate ways.

I only know that he's depressed because my sister told me he posted something about it online.

I don't know if I should bring it up or let it go.

My cousin is addicted to drugs.

And I don't know what to do about it.

I see her a few times a year at family parties.

We share a few laughs over stuff.

Go to the party, have dinner together, and then go our separate ways.

I only know she's an addict because my mom told me.

I don't know if I should bring it up or let it go.

When a person has a problem that does not affect your relationship with them, are you still obligated to help them?

Should I try to get my co-worker a place to live, even though he has never told me about it?

Should I seek out my depressed friend and tell him it will be alright, even though he never contacted me over it?

Should I get my cousin into rehab, even though she never mentioned it to me?

Or would such action by me be overstepping some boundary in our relationship?

I only see the guy a few hours a week.

I only hung out with him at lunch.

I only see her at Christmas.

The type of help they need is only for those closest to the person.

In other words, not me.

What should I do?

I don't know.

I truly don't know.

My Co-Worker Doesn't Get My Shakespeare References

As I work, I get bored of the menial task that does not challenge my mind, and only puts a strain on my body.

My bored mind wanders when I'm alone, which keeps me getting through the day.

I don't think about work, as I do it, I just do it.

Thinking of work only reminds me I'm working.

I ignore all the frustration I feel of being overworked and underpaid.

Those destructive ideas bring nothing but anger to me, so I have learned to restrain them from my work habit.

When I am with another worker, and we get to talking, the writer in me comes out, and I make references that are too much for my co-worker.

Fair is foul…

I expect my co-worker to finish the line.

But he doesn't.

He continues to think of the job.

Some are born great…

Once again nothing.

He may have even thought it was my original line.

And he continues to think of the job.

Nothing will come from nothing.

The guys never read, which is not hyperbole.

He doesn't.

All he thinks of is the job.

We get to talking about movies and other areas of pop culture, and somehow we get to *The Lion King*.

"That is *Hamlet* with animals.

And you know, not everyone dies at the end."

"No. It's not."

He states as if it is a fact.

"Yes. it Is."

"No. It's not."

And that ends that conversation.

This is why I'd prefer to work alone.

Waiting For My Mattress

I sit in my living room waiting for my new mattress.

I've been sleeping on the couch the past week.

Which is honestly, not as bad as you would think.

I mattress is supposed to be here between 2 PM to 6 PM

Or 9:00 to 12:00.

I got two messages about the delivery.

I am going with the earliest and latest times.

I took a moment to reflect.

Is this worth even writing?

Not that its quality is bad or not.

Is it, important?

Plato wrote about philosophical ideas he thought were the most important topics ever.

He wouldn't write this.

But isn't sleep important?

I need it to function.

We all do.

What are any of us without sleep?

Coffee and energy drinks can only do so much.

You need to sleep afterwhile.

I'm talking in a clear sense you have to sleep.

Your body demands it.

Did you know that you could die from lack of sleep?

Really, look it up.

That's how important sleep is; it is life or death.

Granted the battle between the two is slower than a senior with a back problem walking down a crowded aisle, but it still wages on.

So why can't waiting for a mattress be important?

So there is no allegory.

No method.

No trial.

Only me sitting in my living room.

I don't want to hear about me waiting for a mattress as unimportant, as we all struggle with our own sleep habits.

Acknowledgments

I'd like to thank my assistant Angel, and my illustrator Yuzhar Ramadan, and my book cover artist, Leslie T. for helping me produce this book.

I'd also like to thank my family for supporting me as I write it.

About The Author

Greg Luti is an editor, author, poet and blogger. He runs the literary blog Pens and Words. Collected Poems is his first poetry book.

Further Reading

Keep an eye out for Greg Luti's next book, a short story collection, Everything Must Go.